NOTHING
TO FEAR

NOTHING TO FEAR

Jackie French Koller

Gulliver Books
Harcourt Brace Jovanovich, Publishers
San Diego   New York   London

HBJ

Requests for permission to make copies of any
part of the work should be mailed to:
Permissions Department,
Harcourt Brace Jovanovich, Publishers,
Orlando, Florida 32887.

Library of Congress Cataloging-in-Publication Data
Koller, Jackie French.
Nothing to fear/by Jackie French Koller.
p.   cm.
"Gulliver books."
Summary: When his father moves away to find work and his
mother becomes ill, Danny struggles to help his family
during the Great Depression.
ISBN 0-15-200544-7
[1. Family life—Fiction.   2. Depressions—1929—Fiction.]
I. Title.
PZ7.K833No   1991
[Fic]—dc20   90–39344

Designed by Lydia D'moch
Printed in the United States of America

First edition
A   B   C   D   E

To Mom,
with love

Author's Note

On Thursday, October 24, 1929, the New York Stock Exchange crashed. There was no broken glass, no splintered wood, no crumbling concrete—for it was not the building that came tumbling down, but the numbers on the ticker tape inside, numbers that held the key to the economic stability of the United States. The rubble that was left in the wake of that crash was a rubble of human lives and spirits, for by 1932 almost forty percent of white Americans and fifty-six percent of black Americans were without jobs or any source of regular income.*

The children who grew up during the decade that followed, the decade known as the Great Depression, would be forever scarred by the poverty, despair, and humiliation that pervaded our society during those hard times.

My mother was one of those children. Abandoned by her father at the height of the depression, she was

*Brother, Can You Spare a Dime, by Milton Meltzer. New York: Alfred A. Knopf, 1969.

vii

raised along with her brother and seven sisters by my grandmother, a valiant little Irishwoman who often supported her family on little more than the sheer strength of her love.

During my growing-up years, stories of those hard times were told and retold at family gatherings, but they were never told with bitterness. They were told, instead, with all the warmth and laughter of a family made closer and stronger by adversity. It is the indomitable spirit of that family that inspired this book, and if anyone should notice that the Rileys, who pop in and out of its pages with regularity, bear a striking resemblance to the Hayeses who lived at 1444 Park Avenue in New York City in the year 1932, I wouldn't be the least bit surprised.

—*Jackie French Koller*

ONE

Tuesday, October 18, 1932

I'm not gonna pretend like I'm no angel or anything. I mean, I've been in trouble before. But nothing bad. Just small-time stuff, like stealing apples from the carts down around 105th or sneaking into the Bijou over on Lexington without paying my dime. Like I said, small-time stuff. Of course there was that time that Maggie Riley and I dressed a rag doll up in her baby sister's clothes and threw it off the roof. Whew! I can still feel the shellackin' I got for that one. But we were just kids then and we didn't mean any harm. I mean, we never would've done it if we knew her ma was sitting on the fire escape. I felt really bad afterwards. Maggie said she'd never seen her ma faint before, and with nine kids I guess she must've had a scare or two in her time.

But still, that wasn't anything like the mess I got into over at Weissman's market today. I was looking at the penny jar in Weissman's display window when along came the Sullivan twins. They stopped and started arguing with each other about how many pennies there were. I was kind of laughing to myself because I had scientifically figured out how many there were, and I knew I was going to win the contest. I told them they weren't even close, but they wouldn't believe me.

Then Harry, he's the older one—by two minutes I think—came up with the idea to swipe a few licorice whips. He dared me to go in and keep old man Weissman busy in the back room while he and Frank ran in, grabbed a handful, and ran out again. Well, I was kind of hungry myself, and I figured Weissman would never miss a few licorice whips, so I took Harry up on it. I should've known better though. No sooner did I get Weissman into the back room than we heard this big crash. By the time we got out front there was a brick through the display window, and the penny jar was gone. And there was nobody in sight except for Mrs. Ruiz who was standing over by the Campbell's Soup display, shrieking like she'd been shot. I guess I should've just stood there calm and collected and not let on like I knew anything. But when I heard that screaming and saw all that broken glass, I got so scared I just lit out of there like a cat with a bulldog on its tail.

Just my luck, a crowd had already gathered outside, and making his way through the middle of it was Sergeant Finnegan. He seemed to just reach out and grab me from about ten feet away. I guess that's what they mean by the long arm of the law. Anyhow, he's got a pretty good grip for an old guy. I mean, he's got to be at least thirty. He hauled me up short and lifted me by the back of my jacket and I just sort of dangled there like a stupid scarecrow. Then he narrowed his eyes at me and said, "Now where do you think you're goin' in such a hurry, Danny boy?"

That's when I knew I was in for it. Boy was I scared. I felt like I was gonna upchuck any minute. I kept looking for a way out, but I couldn't see any. Sergeant Finnegan had a real good grip on my collar, and even if I did manage to get away, where would I go? Down to the train yard with the hoboes? I had to go home sooner or later, so I figured I might just as well face the music. Besides, it didn't seem like Sergeant Finnegan was gonna give me any choice.

"I oughta haul you right down to the station and scare some sense into you," he said. "If I wasn't such good friends with your pa I'd do just that; but knowin' Daniel Garvey like I do, I think I'll take you on home and let him deal with you."

I felt like saying, "Thanks for nothing," but I figured I'd better just keep my big mouth shut.

You see, you have to know my pa. He's Irish. I mean, right off the boat. And he's got this thing about right and wrong. To hear him tell it, he must've been some goody two shoes when he was a kid. *When I was your age I did this. When I was your age I did that.* Anyhow, he makes this big deal about our name.

3

I guess Garvey's as good a name as any, but to hear him talk you'd think it was dipped in fourteen-karat gold or something.

"Your name is Daniel Tomas Garvey," he always tells me. "It's my name, it was my daddy's name, and it was his daddy's name before him. It's a good name. And that's the one thing no one can ever take away from you."

Sometimes I feel like if he tells me that one more time I'm gonna throw up. Don't get me wrong—it's not that Pa is a bad guy. Most times I'd take him over any other pa I know. It's just that when he thinks our name's been sullied, watch out.

Truth is, I don't much like sullying, either. I don't do it on purpose. Something just comes over me sometimes, and the next thing you know, I've sullied again. It's getting to be a problem.

"Let's go, Danny," said Sergeant Finnegan, giving me a shove.

"Hey," I told him. "I live down on Park."

"I know where you live," Sergeant Finnegan reminded me, "but I've got my beat to finish, so we'll be takin' a little stroll." He gave me a sarcastic smile. "It's a lovely evenin' for a stroll, don't ya think?"

I frowned and didn't answer, and Sergeant Finnegan's smile disappeared.

"Get on with you then," he said, giving me another shove. We walked three blocks north on Madison, then turned east on 110th. It was getting dusky and the streetlights were just starting to come on. All up and down the street men were hanging out on the stoops, just talking and smoking like they do every evening.

The gutter was full of kids playing potsy and jump rope and kick-the-can. The trolley went by and the kids parted in front of it, then closed right in behind again. A bunch of guys on skates grabbed onto the back of the trolley and got pulled along for a while, laughing and screaming, until the conductor shooed 'em off. Overhead, I could hear mothers leaning out of windows and calling their kids and husbands in for supper. I would've given anything to trade places with one of those kids, just going home for an ordinary supper tonight.

Sergeant Finnegan didn't seem to be in any hurry. He stopped to buy an apple from a street vendor.

"How's it going, Joe?" I heard him ask the vendor.

"Been better . . . been worse . . . ," the man said. His voice sounded so flat and hopeless that I turned to have a good look at him. He had straggly hair and a couple of days' growth of beard. A worn overcoat hung from his shoulders, and he stared at the ground when he talked and shuffled from one foot to the other. Something about him reminded me of Mr. Smey, the vice principal from over at PS 72, where I used to go to grammar school. Then he looked up a moment and I realized that he *was* Mr. Smey. Wow! I knew they were laying off teachers left and right, but I had no idea they were letting vice principals go, too. I knew he hadn't recognized me, and I knew he'd rather I didn't recognize him, so I turned away. It was sad, though, to see him with that sign around his neck: Unemployed—Buy an Apple—5 cents.

Sergeant Finnegan stuck his apple in his pocket and we started moving along again. When we finally reached the corner the elevated train rumbled by on its way uptown, and I looked up at it. It runs right up the middle of Park Avenue just about even with our third-story apartment windows, so I've been watching it come and go all my life. I lifted my hand out of habit and waved at the caboose.

Sergeant Finnegan chuckled. "Bet you wish you were on that train about now. Huh, Danny boy?" he said.

I shrugged, not about to let on that he'd just read my mind.

We headed south, back toward my block, and I turned my face to the street, hoping none of the neighbors would recognize me. I stared at a pair of horses who clomped alongside me pulling a heavy cart. Just before my block they turned into the 107th Street tunnel, headed for the stables on the other side of the tracks. I glanced back up Park, afraid Pa might be out on our stoop. Turns out I couldn't see anyway, though, 'cause a big crowd was standing in front of 1446, the building next to ours. A chill ran up my back. Somebody was getting evicted again. That was the third eviction on our block this month. Seems like they're averaging one a week now. Little by little all our friends and neighbors are getting thrown out.

When we got closer I could see that this time it

was Luther White's family. Luther is in the eighth grade with me over at Patrick Henry Junior High. We always give him a hard time because his pa is black and his ma is white, and to top it off, his name is White. "Poor Luther," we always kid, "he don't know if he's black or white."

He never gets mad or anything. He just calls us micks and spics and stuff like that and maybe takes a swat at us. That's the good thing about Luther. He can take a joke.

Luther's pa has been out of work longer than most. He used to be a doorman down at one of those swanky midtown hotels, and right after the stock market crash, as soon as jobs started getting scarce, they took his job and gave it to a white guy. It's happened to a lot of black folks I know.

Seems like the whole city went crazy after that crash. There were people killing themselves—jumping out of windows and off rooftops, throwing themselves into the river. I asked Pa why anyone would kill themselves over something like that. He said money does strange things to people. I guess he's right. Look what that stupid jar of pennies did to me today.

Sergeant Finnegan yanked me to a stop when he saw what was going on out in the street. He let go of my collar and said, "You wait right here, Danny, and behave yourself." Then he gave me a look that put any thoughts of making a break for it right out of my head. He walked on over to Luther's father, tipped his hat, and said, "Afternoon, Luther." Luther's pa is named Luther, too.

"Aftanooon Off'suh Finnegan," said Luther's pa.

He's from down south and he talks like that, kinda drawn out, soft, and slow. I love to hear him talk. Lots of black folks talk like that around here. They moved up from the South when I was little, some even before that. There were plenty of jobs then and the city was full of laughin' and music. I remember on warm summer nights Pa used to walk with me and Ma up to 125th and Lenox to watch the rich folks going into the Cotton Club, and listen to the jazzy sounds coming out. Ma won't let us go up to that part of Harlem at night anymore. She says it's an angry, desperate place now.

"What's the problem here, Luther?" Sergeant Finnegan was asking Luther's pa.

"Just what it 'pears off'suh," Luther's pa told him. "They's puttin' us out."

The sergeant and Mr. White went on talking for a bit. Meanwhile folks were kinda looking over the furniture and stuff on the sidewalk. Luther's ma sat in the middle of it on an old kitchen chair. Luther's baby sister, Rhetta, was on her lap, and Luther's other two sisters hung onto either side of her skirt. She held her chin high and stared straight ahead, ignoring the vultures that were picking through her worldly goods. She looked like she could've been having tea with the queen of England. It made me proud just to look at her.

"All right there, move along, move along!" shouted Sergeant Finnegan. He banged his club on the end of the iron bed and the vultures stepped back and hovered, waiting for a chance to close in again.

"Go on down to St. Cecilia's," Sergeant Finnegan told Luther's pa. "They'll put you up for a day or two, until you can figure what to do."

Luther's pa nodded sadly to Sergeant Finnegan, and the two men shook hands. Then Sergeant Finnegan went over and gave his apple to little Rhetta. I guess maybe he ain't such a bad guy . . . for a cop.

"Come on, Danny," he said, grabbing my collar again. "Let's get on with it."

Luther was just coming down the steps of his front stoop as we went by. He had a ratty old leather satchel in his hand. We looked at each other for a second, then we both looked away. I don't know which of us was more ashamed.

TWO

Pa wasn't down on the stoop, thank goodness, but a bunch of little Rileys were, watching the goings-on next door. At least they didn't have to worry about getting evicted. Their mother is the janitor and they get their rent free. They stared at Sergeant Finnegan with big eyes as we went by. Little Dotty grabbed her doll out of its shoe box and hugged it tight as if she was afraid he might arrest it or something. I said "Boo!" to her and she jumped about three feet.

Sergeant Finnegan yanked my collar.

"That make you feel like a big man, does it?" he asked. "Scaring little girls?"

"No sir," I mumbled, feeling even dumber than I did already.

"Get on with you then . . . and mind your manners."

Inside, the front hall smelled of Lysol. Mrs. Riley

is forever swishing Lysol all over everything. I don't really mind, though. I been in a lot of buildings that smell like stuff I wouldn't care to mention. Our building may not be fancy, but it's always clean. Those Riley kids work like a little army, shining woodwork, washing windows, scrubbing floors. The only one in their family who don't lift a finger is their old man, and Marion, of course, but she's got an excuse. She's only a year and a half old.

I took a quick look at the mailboxes on the wall. The mail was still in 3B. That meant Pa wasn't home yet most likely. My heart gave a little leap. Maybe Sergeant Finnegan wouldn't be able to wait.

Sergeant Finnegan went to push the bell next to our box.

"You don't have to do that," I told him. "The lock's busted." I pushed the inside door open and we started up the steps. There was a big commotion overhead, and Maggie Riley and her sister Kitty came clattering down the steps swinging the coal bucket between them. They stopped short when they saw us and flattened themselves against the wall as we went by. Maggie rolled her eyes at me, then I heard her and Kitty whispering and giggling behind us as they started back down the steps. Girls!

Ma was singing. We could hear her clear down to the first landing. She sings real pretty. I read in a book once about this bird that could sing so beautiful that it made some Chinese emperor cry. It was called a nightingale. I think Ma must sing like a nightingale. Pa says her singing puts him in mind of the green hills of home, meaning Ireland. He says that when our ship comes in we're gonna buy Ma a piano.

Ma sings while she does the ironing. She says it makes the hours fly—and she spends a lot of hours ironing. She takes in the washing for a fancy ladies' hotel down on Eighty-Ninth Street. She used to be the cleaning lady there before my baby sister, Maureen, was born. That's how she got the laundry job.

Pa's always teasing her about it. He says, "Molly, sure an' they'll be writin' on yer tombstone, Here Lies Molly Garvey and her Iron. We Couldna' Pry It from her Hand."

Pa talks like that on account of he's right off the boat, like I said. So is Mama. I was born here—in New York—but I used to talk like them, too, until I went to school and learned good English like I talk now.

When we got to our door, Sergeant Finnegan pulled his hat off and held it in his two hands kind of respectful-like. Then he yanked my cap off and made me hold it, too, like we were going to church or something. Mama has that effect on people.

There was some kind of ruckus going on in the Rileys' apartment across the hall. Sounded like old man Riley was spifflicated again. Somewhere upstairs somebody was cooking cabbage. I could tell because the cabbage stink was floating down and fighting with the Lysol stink for control of the hall.

Sergeant Finnegan didn't pay any attention to the ruckus or the stinks. He just went ahead and knocked on our door.

The singing stopped and Ma called out, "Aye, who is it?"

Sergeant Finnegan cleared his throat. "It's me, Miz Garvey," he called back, "Mike Finnegan. I brung Danny home."

There was a scuffling inside, then the door flew open and Ma stood there staring at me wild-eyed, like she expected to see me covered with blood or something. When she saw that I was all in one piece, she let out a big sigh and gave me a look like I had wounded her mortal soul.

"Oh, Danny," she said. "What've ya been up to now?"

I just stood there twisting my cap and staring at my shoes until Sergeant Finnegan escorted me in the door.

"Daniel home yet, Miz Garvey?" he asked.

"No," said Mama, "but I'll be expectin' him any minute. Won't ya sit down, Michael?"

Sergeant Finnegan pulled out a kitchen chair and sat down, one leg bent under the rungs, the other sticking straight out like it was made of wood. Obviously he meant to stay and talk to Pa, which didn't thrill me too much. I looked around the room. All the statues and crucifixes and pictures of Jesus and Mary seemed to be staring right at me, their eyes full of sorrow, like I'd broken their hearts. I felt really hot all of a sudden. I tossed my cap onto the icebox, then pulled off my jacket and threw it over a hook by the door.

Mama's ironing board was set up over by the stove

with a half-ironed tablecloth hanging off it. Behind that, in the tub, another load of wash was soaking in bluing, and outside the window, just beyond the fire escape, a bunch of sheets were flapping in the wind. Folks say nothing's sure in life but death and taxes, but Pa says in our house you can count on one more thing—laundry.

Maureen sat on a blanket in the middle of the floor taking the coffeepot apart. She was so interested in what she was doing, she hadn't even seen us come in. Her breath came out in little puffs, and a line of drool dripped from her bottom lip.

"Hey, Mo," I whispered.

She looked up and smiled a big grin when she saw me.

"Da!" she said, clapping her little hands together. That's what she calls me—Da, just like she's trying to say Dan, but she can't quite get the *n* out.

She decided to get up off the blanket. She just learned how to do it, so it takes her a while. She sort of leans forward on her hands, then gets her legs under her and pushes her little bottom up. Then she straightens up quick and sort of balances there a minute with a surprised look on her face. Sometimes she tumbles back down at that point and has to start all over again, but this time she made it.

"Da," she said, "Da . . . ," toddling over and putting her hands up to me.

To tell the truth I was real glad to have something to do. I picked her up and gave her a hug.

She's a bonny little thing, and I love her a lot. I didn't think I was ever gonna have any brothers and sisters because Mama doesn't do too good at having babies. She lost a few between me and Maureen, but by the time Maureen came along we had money enough for a hospital. Mama was pretty sick for a while, but everything turned out okay.

I buried my nose in Maureen's neck. It smelled like the cotton candy they sell down at Coney Island. She giggled and stuck her finger in my mouth.

Mama was flitting around the kitchen like a canary with a cat peeking in its cage. She picked the blanket and the coffeepot up off the floor. She lugged the laundry and the ironing board back into the spare room. She pushed the irons to the back of the stove and put the kettle on, and she kept apologizing for the mess, which there wasn't any of. I know she was dying to know what I'd done, but I guess she was afraid to ask.

Sergeant Finnegan kept pulling on his collar like it was too tight as he tried to make small talk. Then he brought up the Whites.

Mama stopped flitting and dropped heavily into the chair across from him. She pulled a handkerchief from her housedress pocket and twisted it in her hands.

"Oh, Michael," she said, "what's to become of them?"

Sergeant Finnegan shrugged and shook his head. "Have they got family?" he asked.

"Not on Anna's side," Mama said. "Her folks have

had nothin' to do with her since she married Luther. I s'pose they could head back down south where Luther's from . . ."

Sergeant Finnegan snorted. "Not if they're smart," he said. "Luther'll get himself lynched looking for work down there. Just read in the paper today about a mob of whites that pulled some poor colored railroad worker off a train and shot him dead, just to get his job. And that ain't the first one I've heard of, either."

Mama's face went pale with horror. She shook her head.

"I feel so guilty," she said, "not offerin' to take them in. But what would I feed them . . . and . . . Lord only knows . . ."

She glanced up at me quick and didn't say anything more. I knew what she was thinking—Lord only knows how much longer we'll be able to pay the rent. With Pa out of work and the savings all gone, how much longer could we survive on Ma's ironing money and the little bit I bring in shining shoes?

The kettle started to whistle and Ma got up to fix tea. Downstairs I heard the heavy thud of the front door banging shut and my belly started to ache again. I hugged Maureen tighter and waited.

THREE

They were Pa's footsteps all right. I could just see him dragging his heavy feet up the stairs, his overcoat sagging from his shoulders, his eyes dark and broody like the sea before a storm.

Pa don't look like the rest of us, with his black, wavy hair and eyes to match. Me and Maureen take after Ma. I sure wish I did look like Pa, though. Not that Ma isn't pretty or anything, it's just that red hair and freckles look better on a lady, I think. Like Maureen. She's cute as the dickens, but me . . . well, I just can't see that women are ever gonna look at me the way I've seen 'em look at Pa. "Handsome as the devil!" That's what they always say.

Usually Pa's footsteps grow quicker and lighter when they reach our landing. Just outside our door he stops and straightens up and plasters on a big smile. I watched him do it one day when I was sitting on the fourth-floor landing and he didn't know I was there. Then he opens the door and walks in just like everything is hunky-dory. Then Ma and I plaster on big smiles and pretend everything's hunky-dory, too, even though it isn't.

It isn't like when Pa was working. He's a carpenter, and up until March of last year he was building the Empire State Building. He used to fly up the stairs two at a time then, whistling an Irish jig. He'd burst in all full of news and scoop Mama up and make her giggle. Then he'd run on and on at supper.

"Another story today," he'd say. "Would ya believe, a story a day? Three thousand men on one job! Ah, 'tis a glory ta see."

Then after dinner he'd light his pipe and sit back with his newspaper. When he first came to this country, he went to school nights to learn to read, and ever since then he's considered it his bounden duty to keep up with the news.

"Your daddy was a poor farm boy back in Ireland," he used to tell me, holding his pipe bowl in his hand and pointing the stem at me. "Couldna' even read! Now he's buildin' the tallest buildin' in the whole world. Ah, America—'tis truly the land of opportunity."

Pa doesn't say much about the land of opportunity anymore. He doesn't say much at all. He just gets up every morning, shaves and washes like always, then goes out and walks from one end of the city to the other, looking for work. Sometimes he goes down to the New York City Free Employment Bureau and stands in line, fighting with five thousand other guys for the handful of jobs that come in every day. Once in a while he even takes my shoeshine box and goes out on the streets. He doesn't want me to know that, but I saw him one day, down on his knees, shining some guy's shoes—my daddy, my strong, proud daddy that can read the newspaper and build the tallest building in the world, down on his knees in the gutter. I never let on to him that I saw.

The footsteps didn't get light and quick this time, and there was no plastered-on smile when Pa pushed the door open. I stood staring at him, my hands all sweaty, my heart flopping around like a fish out of water.

"Hi, Pa," I said, my voice coming out in a squeak. I held Maureen out in front of me like a shield. She reached for him with both hands, and he smiled a little in spite of himself and scooped her out of my arms. He shot me a glance, though, that let me know he'd gotten the word from the men down on the street.

He walked over and gave Mama a quick kiss. Then he put Maureen in her lap and turned to Sergeant Finnegan.

"Evenin', Michael," he said, extending his hand stiffly. "I take it yer not here on a social call?"

"No, Daniel, I'm afraid not."

Well, Sergeant Finnegan launched into the whole story then, and Pa just stood there taking it all in. I could tell he was gettin' sore though, because of his nostrils. When Ma gets mad her face turns so red that her freckles all run together and her green eyes flash like lightning. But when Pa gets mad his eyes turn hard and cold as ice, and his nostrils flare out like a wild stallion's.

Ma kept giving me mournful glances, and when Sergeant Finnegan got to the part about the broken window and the stolen money she said, "Oh, dear God," and crossed herself like she was trying to ward off the devil.

Pa turned and looked at me and my insides froze solid.

"Daniel."

"Yes sir."

"Come here."

My shoes turned into lead and it took all my strength to drag them across the floor.

"Were you in on this, Daniel? I want the truth."

I sure wanted to say no, but it was no use. When Pa looks into my eyes like that I swear he can see right into my brain.

"They said they were just gonna grab some licorice whips," I blurted. "I didn't know they were gonna break the window . . . honest."

Pa's eyes narrowed. "And just who'll *they* be?" he asked.

I stared down at the linoleum. If there's one thing I ain't, it's a stool pigeon.

Pa grabbed my chin and made me look at him again.

"*Who,* Danny?"

I kept staring at him. My mouth dried out and I

got this lump in my throat that wouldn't go down, but I still didn't say anything.

Pa put his nose right on top of mine and yelled into my mouth. "Do you know what a window like that'll be costin'?"

He yelled it so loud I probably would've fallen over if it weren't for my lead shoes.

"Do ya?"

"No sir."

"More'n we've got, and more'n poor Weissman has got, either."

"Poor Weissman?" I said, suddenly finding my voice. "Aw, c'mon, Pa, everybody knows the old guy is loaded."

That *really* did it. I don't know which Pa hates worse, talking back or being disrespectful to elders—but it didn't matter, 'cause I'd just managed to do them both in one sentence. His eyes bugged out, and for a minute I thought he was gonna wallop me right then and there.

Instead he just stood there breathing hard, with his eyes burning into mine for what seemed like about ten thousand years. Then he sucked in a deep breath, pushed me aside, and turned back to Sergeant Finnegan.

"Thank you for yer trouble, Michael," he said, nodding stiffly. "I'll see to it things are put right."

"I know you will, Daniel," said Sergeant Finnegan. Then he picked up his hat, nodded to Mama, and left.

21

We listened to his footsteps going down the stairs, the silence growing heavier and heavier in the room. Finally, with the thud of the front door, Pa turned back to me.

"Get yer coat," he said. "We're goin' out."

"Where'll you be taking him?" Ma asked anxiously.

"To see Weissman," Pa told her. "You'd best have yer supper and feed Maureen. There's no knowin' how long we'll be, and speakin' fer m'self, I've no appetite anyway."

Mama bit her lip and nodded sadly. Pa snatched my cap off the icebox and shoved it at me, then he walked out the door. I looked at Ma and her eyes started to get all shiny and wet, so I pulled the cap down low over my eyes, grabbed my jacket, and beat it out the door after Pa.

FOUR

Pa didn't say a word all the way over to Weissman's market. I walked a little behind him, hurrying to keep up. I wanted so bad to talk to him, but his big back was like a wall, shutting me out.

When we got there Mr. Weissman was gone and the sign on the door said CLOSED. There were some old boards nailed up on the inside of the window and another cop was standing on the sidewalk watching to see that nobody tried to break in. The hole in the glass looked open and ugly, like a giant wound. I almost expected to see blood on the sidewalk.

Pa walked over and talked quietly to the cop. The cop stared at me over his shoulder, and my face grew hot as a branding iron. I wondered if Pa was gonna have him haul me down to the station after all. The cop mumbled a few words back to Pa then pointed south down Madison Avenue. Pa thanked him and took off again without a word to me.

"Pa?" I called after him, but he didn't answer. I stared at the cop, not sure what I was supposed to do. The cop made no move to arrest me or anything, so I shoved my hands in my pockets and hightailed it after Pa.

We walked all the way down to 102d, then Pa stopped outside of an apartment house that looked a lot like ours. Of course, most of the brownstones in our part of the city look pretty much alike. Some have fire escapes in the front, some have 'em in the back. That's about the only difference I can see. I wondered why we were stopping at this one.

"Pa?" I said again.

He still didn't answer. He walked up the steps, pulled the door open, and went inside. The door slammed behind him and there I was again, by myself. I looked up and down the street. It was pretty quiet, except for the usual bums hanging about in the alleyways. A couple of fellas were standing on the corner under the streetlight, smoking cigarettes. They started to laugh and I got this crazy idea that they knew who I was and what I'd done and they were laughing at me. So I beat it up the stairs and into the building.

The front hall was empty, and I stood there for a minute, wondering what to do. It was just like our front hall, with dark wood paneling and a black-and-white tiled floor. There was no light in it, but the light from the inside hall shone dimly through the pebbled-glass door. I figured Pa must've gone inside, so I pushed on the door. The lock was broken, like ours. I wasn't surprised. It's hard to keep locks on buildings anymore with all the vagrants so desperate for places to sleep.

I stepped inside and looked quickly around. I hate hallways at night. The little bare bulbs on each floor are just enough to cast deep shadows into every nook and corner, making great hiding places for who-knows-who and who-knows-what. I could hear footsteps overhead, so I shot up the stairs, hoping they were Pa's. I caught up with him on the fourth floor. The building was exactly like ours, with one apartment to the left of the landing and one to the right, and the toilet straight ahead. Seeing the toilet made me realize that I had to go, but it was pitch-dark in there. Not that ours is any different. Folks always swipe the light bulbs out of the toilets 'cause they're easy to reach. Your own toilet is scary enough, though, let alone some stranger's. I decided I could wait.

Pa was knocking on 4B. He motioned for me to come over, then he yanked my cap off and handed it to me just like Sergeant Finnegan had done that afternoon. It was starting to make me mad. I mean, I'm no dummy. I can take my own hat off.

There was some scraping and shuffling inside the apartment, then the latch slid over and the door opened a crack. A tiny, white-haired woman peered out.

"Yes?" she said, her voice quivering a little.

"Mrs. Weissman?" asked Pa.

"Yes."

Mrs. Weissman? I couldn't believe my ears. Why would the Weissmans be living in a cold-water flat with all their dough?

"Could we come in a moment, ma'am?" Pa was asking.

The woman's eyebrows knit together. "We've got no food to spare," she said. "You'd best be on your way." She started to close the door again, but Pa put his foot in the way.

"Please, ma'am," he begged. "I'm not lookin' fer no handouts. The name's Garvey, Daniel Garvey, and this be m'son, Danny. We come to make amends, about the window."

Mrs. Weissman's eyes widened and she stared at Pa a moment, then beyond him, at me. She searched my face gravely, like a judge deciding a verdict, then she nodded and pulled the door open.

"Come in," she said quietly.

She hobbled ahead of us in worn slippers over to a table where Mr. Weissman sat eating. He had on an old sweater with the elbows patched and one of those funny little hats that look like a ball cut in half. He didn't look like a rich man. His apartment didn't look like a rich man's, either. Except for the lack of holy pictures and crucifixes, it could have been ours. There was an old coal stove, a wooden icebox, and not much else. The curtains were thin and faded, and the linoleum was worn through in spots. Even the oilcloth on the table was old and frayed. I wondered what the Weissmans did with all their money.

26

Mr. Weissman went right on eating, taking no notice of us.

"Papa," said Mrs. Weissman, "we have guests."

Mr. Weissman glanced up briefly, then his eyes disappeared again under his bushy white eyebrows.

"A guest, I invite," he snarled.

"Papa," Mrs. Weissman pleaded, "they come to make amends."

The old man snorted. "I have no time for hoodlums," he grumbled. "Go away and let me eat my supper in peace."

I glanced at Pa. He wasn't saying anything, but his eyes were hard and I knew it was killing him to hear a Garvey called a hoodlum.

I cleared my throat.

"Mr. Weissman," I said, my face burning, "I know what I did was wrong, but I ain't no hoodlum. Those guys said they were just gonna grab some licorice whips. It was supposed to be a prank. I didn't mean no harm."

Mr. Weissman looked up and pulled on his beard. He didn't look convinced.

"Tell me the names of the other boys, then," he said.

I stared at the floor.

Mr. Weissman snorted. "So, honor among thieves, is it?" He laughed.

"I'm no thief!"

Mr. Weissman's eyebrows crashed together. He leaned forward and pounded his fist on the table. "A thief is a thief!" he shouted. "A licorice whip today, an apple tomorrow. What next? A pretty toy? A woman's purse?"

"I'd never take anything like that," I answered angrily.

"No? Then why do you protect those who do?"

I looked down at the floor again.

"As they say, thicker than thieves . . ." Mr. Weissman smirked.

"I'm no thief!"

"So you say, so you say." Mr. Weissman waved my words away, then he pointed a finger at me and his face turned red with fury. "No matter," he shouted. "I know who did it, and one day I'll catch the little momzers!"

"Papa!" said Mrs. Weissman sharply. "Watch your tongue. The *child!*"

Mr. Weissman snorted and looked back down at his plate and mumbled something under his breath. I wasn't too thrilled about Mrs. Weissman calling me a child, but I guessed it was better than the names Mr. Weissman was mumbling.

"Come, sit," Mrs. Weissman said. "Papa's bark is worse than his bite."

"Thank you, ma'am," said Pa, "but . . ."

"Sit, sit," insisted the old woman. "We'll have some tea, then we'll talk."

Pa nodded his thanks and sat down. He motioned for me to do the same, and I slid into the chair on the other side of the table. We sat in silence while Mr. Weissman went on with his supper—some watery-looking soup, a crumbly loaf of bread, and a bowl of fruit that looked well past its prime.

Mrs. Weissman brought over two glasses filled with steaming tea and put them down in front of Pa and me.

"Here," she said, pushing the bowl of fruit at me. "Eat."

I eyed one of the oranges eagerly. Mr. Weissman suddenly threw his hands in the air and started talking to the ceiling.

"Such a woman you give me," he shouted. "She invited thieves to my table, and now she wants to *feed* them?"

Pa shot me a sharp glance and I pushed the bowl away. "Tea'll be fine, thanks," I told Mrs. Weissman.

She gave her husband an angry look, but she sat down and said nothing more.

"Mr. Weissman," said Pa, "I'd like to be payin' for the window. . . ." Pa's voice faltered, and Mr. Weissman looked up and regarded him through narrowed eyes.

"I . . . I've got no money with me," Pa went on, "but I could have it to you by Saturday."

Mr. Weissman arched an eyebrow, then he sat back again and pulled at his wiry white beard. He looked Pa and me up and down slowly.

"You've a wife, Mr. Garvey?" he asked.

"Aye. You know her, I think. She comes into the store—Molly Garvey's her name."

"Ah, yes," said Mr. Weissman. "And a baby girl, too. Am I right?"

"Aye."

"And are they well fed, Mr. Garvey?"

Pa's face flushed red. "What're ya drivin' at, man?" he said sharply.

Mr. Weissman leaned forward, both hands on the table. "Just this, Garvey. Keep your money, and keep your boy outa my store. Things like this have happened before. They'll happen again. I'll manage."

Pa's hands clenched tight around his glass. "No," he said evenly, "we Garveys pay our debts."

It just about killed me to see Weissman humiliating Pa like that.

"It's my debt, Pa," I said. "And I'll pay it."

Pa looked at me, and I could see I'd redeemed myself some in his eyes, but he looked doubtful.

"And how're ya plannin' to do that, Danny?" he asked.

I thought for a minute. It didn't make any sense to offer my shoeshine money. We needed that to get by. I said the only other thing I could think of.

"I'll work it off, Pa."

Mr. Weissman burst out laughing.

"Work it off!" he said. "Where? In my store? You hear that, Golda? The fox wants to work in the hen-house."

I could see Pa was getting hot under the collar. "Mr. Weissman," he said, "Danny's a good boy. He's done his share of mischief, but that's behind 'im now."

He paused and looked at me sharply, and I nodded as sincerely as I could.

Pa reached into his pocket and pulled something out and put it on the table. It was Grandfather Garvey's gold watch—his most prized possession.

"You hold this watch," he told Mr. Weissman. "If Danny don't keep to his word, it's yours."

Mr. Weissman picked up the watch. He opened it and read the inscription inside, then he turned it over and examined it carefully. He nodded his appreciation, then dropped the watch into his shirt pocket and patted it. He reached out a hand to Pa. "You have a deal, Mr. Garvey," he said.

Pa took his hand and shook it firmly, then Mr. Weissman turned to his wife and smiled. "Golda," he said, "where are your manners? Offer our guests some fruit."

FIVE

Pa promised Mr. Weissman that I would work every day after school until Christmas to pay off the window and the penny jar. Turns out there was twelve dollars and twenty-three cents in that jar. Boy, does that make me mad. The guess I'd entered in the contest was twelve dollars and thirty-five cents. I probably would've won! I can't wait to get my hands on those Sullivan boys.

When Pa found out that Mr. Weissman kept a spare window-glass in the back room, he insisted on going right down and fixing it. I wanted to go along and help, but Pa wouldn't let me because I hadn't done my homework yet. Pa thinks homework is some kind of a sacred duty, so he sent me on home alone.

I don't like the city at night anymore. There are bums and derelicts everywhere. I know they're mostly just down-and-outers—men like Pa, who've lost their jobs—only looking for a place to sleep. But tonight they all seemed to have that sick gleam in their eyes, like that man a couple of years ago who pulled me into an alley and tried to drag me down a cellar. I'd bitten his hand and gotten away, but I was too scared and too ashamed to tell anyone. A couple of days later they found a kid murdered in that cellar. They never caught that guy, either.

I shivered and put one hand into my pocket, closing it around the handle of the old ice pick I've carried ever since.

"Hey, kid."

The voice startled me. I felt a hand on my shoulder and I whirled around with all my strength, knocking the man off balance. He staggered back against the wall of the building behind us and slid to the ground. I pulled the ice pick from my pocket.

"Please," he whispered hoarsely. His eyes filled with terror as he put his hands up to shield his face. I could see now that he was nothing but a skeleton, pale and sickly.

"Please," he repeated again, "I only wanted a light." He held up an old half-smoked cigarette he must have found in the gutter.

I stuck the ice pick back in my pocket and put out a hand to help him up. "Sorry," I said, feeling like a real jerk.

"No harm done," he mumbled, then added hopefully, "Got a light?"

I fumbled in my pockets. I had a bunch of match covers for playing cards with, but no whole books. "Sorry," I said.

"Could you spare a dime, then?"

I shook my head. "Sorry," I said again. The man nodded matter-of-factly and shuffled off.

When I got home I couldn't quite get up the nerve to go in and face Ma, so I went out the back door into the yard. It's not much of a yard really, just a little patch of fenced-in dirt, but nobody ever goes out there at night, and it's a good place for when you got some thinkin' to do.

Somebody had left their ash bucket out, so I turned it upside down and sat on it, leaning back against the fence. I looked up at the little patch of sky way above the buildings. The moon was out, though I couldn't see it. Just about full, too, judging from the brightness. Clotheslines crisscrossed over my head like the web of a drunken spider, slicing the sky into little wedges.

A shooting star streaked across one of the wedges and was gone so quickly that I wasn't even sure I'd really seen it. I made a wish, just in case. I wished that when I grew up there really would be spaceships, like in that Jules Verne book, *From the Earth to the Moon*, and that one day I'd get to ride in one and see the stars up close. It amazes me to think that the stars and the sky go on forever. I can't picture anything that has no end. Seems to me there's got to be an edge somewhere.

I looked over at the square of yellow that was our

kitchen window. A shadow moved across it—Mama. My heart ached at the thought of the pain I'd caused her. I swore to myself that I'd never hurt her again. I've sworn that before, but this time I meant it—I really, really meant it.

I looked at the other squares of yellow that climbed like ladders up the sides of the buildings. I thought about the people inside, those who are still there. Then I thought about all those who were gone and the others who have come to take their places.

On summer nights when the windows are open, you can listen in on people's lives—babies crying, kids laughing, radios blaring, mothers yelling, couples fighting. Funny thing is, the sounds are always the same. Even though different people come and go, the sounds stay the same. I like that. It makes me feel a part of something big, something never ending, like the stars.

There were no sounds tonight. Only the whistle of the wind coming through the alleys. There's something lonely about October with the summer sounds all gone and the cold winter ahead. I looked over at the empty, black windows of the Whites' apartment, windows that were warm and yellow just yesterday, and I shivered.

The cold was starting to seep through my jacket, and the rim of the old bucket was cutting into my rear. I guessed I couldn't put it off any longer. It was time to go in.

SIX

Once I was inside, the darkness at the back of the hall closed around me and gave me the heebie-jeebies. I hurried up the stairs, pausing at each landing to stare into dark corners for shapes and shadows I really didn't want to see.

At our landing my body reminded me that I still had to go to the toilet. I stared at the dark doorway and waited a few minutes, hoping one or two of the Riley kids would come out. They're lucky. With nine of them they can always find someone else who has to go, then they take turns keeping watch for each other. I couldn't very well drag Maureen out here, and now that I'm thirteen I'm not about to let Ma and Pa know that I'm still scared to go.

The longer I waited, the worse I had to go, so I sucked in my breath, rushed in, and peed just as fast as I could, keeping my eyes glued all the time on the little vent that leads to the air shaft. I've heard all kinds of stories about people climbing down through the air shafts and murdering people in the toilet. In the daytime those stories seem silly—how could anyone climb down that skinny little air shaft? But at night, anything seems possible. I zipped my pants up, paused a minute in the doorway to make sure no one was waiting to grab me, then made a beeline for our apartment.

Maureen was already asleep when I came in, and Mama was ironing again. Only this time she wasn't singing. She didn't even have the radio on. She looked up at me with a pained expression on her face. I sure wished I could wipe it away.

"Where's Pa?" she asked quietly.

"Fixing the window."

She nodded, then went back to her ironing.

I went over and stood awkwardly beside her. She looked up at me again and I could feel tears starting in my eyes, even though I'm too big to cry.

"I didn't mean it to happen, Ma," I blurted. "Honest I didn't."

The pain in Ma's eyes was washed away by forgiveness. She smiled and shook her head and reached her arms out to me. I flew into them like a little kid.

"Oh, Danny," she whispered into my hair, "what're we ta do with you?"

"Nothing, Mama," I told her. "You won't have

to do nothing. I'm never gonna get in trouble again. I promise. You'll see."

She hugged me and kissed the top of my head.

"I hope so, Danny," she said. "Come now. Sit down. I've kept yer supper warm."

She dished me up some vegetable soup and a piece of bread.

"Any butter?" I asked.

"No," she said quietly, "no butter tonight."

"That's okay. I didn't really feel like it anyway," I lied. "Did you eat yet?"

"No, I'm waitin' fer Pa."

I ate the vegetables out, then sopped up the broth with my bread. It was good. I sure would've liked some more. It just seems like I'm hungry all the time lately, like my stomach is a big, empty cave, and I can't ever fill it up. It even aches sometimes. I know better than to ask Mama for seconds, though. If I ask, she'll pretend she isn't hungry and give me her portion.

Pa still wasn't back when I finished my homework. I was kind of glad. I was feeling really tired, and I didn't want to talk about what I'd done any more tonight.

I went back out into the hall. This time there was a whole line of little Rileys waiting to use the toilet. Fortunately Maggie and Kitty weren't there, because I didn't feel like talking to them, either. The little ones stared at me like they were bursting with curiosity, but I just gave 'em all a mean look and they knew enough to keep their traps shut. Little kids are so easy to scare.

I kissed Ma and told her I was going to bed. She nodded and said not to wake Maureen. Our apartment is a railroad flat with all the rooms in a row, opening one into the other like railroad cars, so I have to go through Ma and Pa's room to get to mine. Maureen was sleeping soundly in her crib at the foot of their bed. I kissed my hand and reached through the bars to touch her cheek. She stirred and made little sucking noises with her mouth, like she was drinking her bottle. She was awful cute, lying on her tummy with her little bottom poking up in the air. I pulled her blanket close around her, although it was fairly warm in Ma's room, being so close to the kitchen.

My room comes next, because it's the next warmest. After that comes the spare room and then the front room. If all Ma's babies had been okay, I'd be in the spare room now, or maybe even the front room like Maggie and Kitty Riley. They have to pile every coat in their house on their beds to stay warm at night. Maggie says sometimes she wakes up exhausted, just from the weight.

There's another door in the front room, going out into the hall. When I was little I used to love to chase the Riley girls in a big circle from the kitchen through the bedrooms and the front room, out the front-room door, back in the kitchen door, and round and round again. Sometimes we'd open up the Rileys' doors, and run through their rooms, too. Our mothers never seemed to mind, but when our fathers were home we always got sent outside after once or twice around.

I put on my pajamas, then crept into the front room and peeked out the window. Still no sign of Pa. I heard Riley's front-room door open across the hall, and Maggie and Kitty's voices right outside. I beat it back to bed so they wouldn't know I was there and come barging in. Those Rileys are the worst for barging in any time of the day and night. Their mother has spare keys to all the apartments, so even with the doors locked you're not safe.

I climbed into bed. Saturday, confession day, is a whole three days away, and I hate to go that long with so many sins on my soul in case I get killed or something in between. I decided to try an idea Luther White told me about. He's a Baptist, and he said Baptists confess their sins right straight to God without a priest in the middle. He said it worked okay as far as he knew, and I couldn't see where it would hurt, so I gave it a try.

"Bless me, Father, for I have sinned," I whispered. "These are my sins . . ."

I was only about halfway through the list when I heard Pa come in, so I hurried with the rest and strained to hear what he and Ma were saying. At first all I heard was the clink of their spoons and the slurping of soup, but after a while I saw the lights go out and heard the springs squeak as they climbed into bed. They started to talk then, but their voices were so low and secretive I couldn't hear what they were saying. There was something in the tone that worried me, and I crept out of bed and knelt by the doorway, listening through the curtains we use for a door.

"When?" I heard Ma ask.

"Tomorrow," said Pa.

Ma sucked her breath in sharply. "So soon?" she whispered.

"The sooner the better," said Pa. "I'm nothin' but a burden to ya here."

"Don't say that, Daniel," Mama protested. "You know it isn't true."

"You know what I'm saying, Molly," Pa went on. "There's no jobs to be had in the city, and there won't be. Not for a long time."

"But the election," Mama protested. "Surely Roosevelt will win. Then things'll be changin'."

"Aye, I hope so," said Pa. "But it'll take time, and we've no time left. The whole city is sick—people hungry, homeless, children stealing. . . ."

Mama didn't answer.

"I'll come for you as soon as I've found work," Pa went on. "It'll be grand, Molly. We'll make a new start—find a nice, green place for the children to grow up in."

"But this is our home," said Mama, her voice unsure. "Our friends are here. We don't know anything else, Daniel."

Pa laughed. "Are you forgettin' where ya came

41

from, then? Clear across the ocean. Where's the courage ya had then, lass?"

"That was before the children. Children make a woman more . . . cautious."

"It's *because* of the children that we've got to go, Molly. Can't ya see that? Danny don't know wrong from right anymore, and how can I blame him? His belly's always empty, and I can't do nothin' to fill it. He sees the bootleggers and the hustlers living high off of everyone else's misery, while his poor honest father sits by helpless and watches his own children starve!"

Pa's voice rose and trembled when he said these words.

"Shhh," I heard Ma whisper. I couldn't hear what she was saying anymore, but her voice was calm and soothing.

After a while there was no more talking. I heard Pa breathing regular and slow, like he was asleep. I stretched out on the floor and lay with my face pressed against the cool wood. I felt worse than I'd ever felt in my life. Pa was leaving, and it was all my fault.

Then I heard another sound. Mama was crying.

I don't cry much anymore, not like when I was a little kid. But there's one thing that'll do it to me every time, and that's seeing Mama cry. Even just hearing her was enough. My throat got all choked up and sore, and tears started flooding out of my eyes. I rolled over on my back and stared at the ceiling, trying to make them stop without sniffling out loud. They slid down my cheeks and pooled in my ears, but I didn't wipe them away. I let them stay 'til they dried on my face, itchy and cold. The floor was hard against my back and the dampness of the weekly scrubbing Ma gave it came right through my pajamas. My feet were cold as ice, and my throat ached like I'd swallowed a knife sideways. But I didn't care. I felt like the scum of the earth, and the scum of the earth doesn't deserve any better.

SEVEN

Wednesday, October 19, 1932

I guess I somehow managed to fall asleep that way, because the next thing I knew I felt this thump in my side and I looked up and saw Pa standing over me with a surprised look on his face.

"Danny, what're you doin' on the floor, lad?"

I blinked and rubbed my eyes. I wasn't too sure myself, to tell the truth. I had this vague feeling, though, that something was wrong. Then I remembered.

I looked at Pa. He had on his overcoat, his wool cap, and the scarf Ma had made him last Christmas.

"You're leavin', Pa," I said. I meant it to sound like a question, but it came out like a statement, flat and hopeless.

Pa's eyes were sorrowful. He held a hand out to me.

"You were listenin' last night," he said.

I nodded and took his hand, and he pulled me slowly to my feet. Boy, was I stiff and sore. Now I know what Mrs. Mahoney upstairs means when she complains about her rheumatism.

"Yer shiverin'," said Pa. He led me over to the bed, sat me down, and wrapped my blanket around me.

"What d'ya mean, sleeping on the floor like that?" he scolded. "You'll catch your death—"

"You're going away, Pa," I said again.

Pa sighed and put his arm around my shoulders.

"I got to, Danny. I got to find work."

I remembered all the times when I was small and I would have a nightmare and cry out in the dark, and the next thing I knew, Pa would be by my side. "It's okay, Danny," he would always say. "I'm here." And it was okay, because he was.

"I don't want you to go," I said.

"I don't want to go either, Danny. But I got to." He clapped me on the knee. "Get yerself dressed and you can walk with me a ways."

I put my head down. "Okay," I whispered.

Maureen woke up and yelled and Pa went to get her. I dressed quickly and followed them out into the kitchen. Ma was very quiet. Her eyes were puffy.

"Danny'll be walkin' with me a ways," Pa told her.

"Not 'til he's had some breakfast, he won't."

"Aw, Ma."

"Yer Ma's right," said Pa. "A lad needs his breakfast. There's time."

45

There wasn't *much* time, if I was going to do my shoe shining and still make it to school. I wolfed down my oatmeal in about three gulps, then I jumped up and grabbed my cap. "I'm ready," I said, my mouth still full.

Pa got up and turned to face Mama. "Well," he said.

"Well," said Mama in return.

Pa kissed Maureen and handed her to me, then he pulled Mama into his arms and kissed her hard on the lips. When the kiss was over they looked into each other's eyes.

"Smile for me," said Pa.

Ma's chin quivered, and her eyes were watery, but she managed to curl the corners of her mouth up just a little.

"That's my girl," said Pa, playfully pulling at her chin. "You just keep smilin', and I'll be back before ya know I'm gone."

He picked up the little sack of belongings Ma had put together for him and motioned me to come. "And don't forget yer shoeshine box," he told me. "Yer ma's countin' on that money."

I handed Maureen back to Ma and picked up my box.

"Not too far now," Mama warned. "I don't want you to be late fer school."

"I won't," I promised.

Pa pulled the door open and a furrow creased Mama's brow. "Daniel," she called suddenly.

Pa turned back to look at her. "Aye?"

Ma leaned forward a moment, her mouth open as if to speak, then she shrank back and shook her head.

"Just . . . God be with you."

"And with you, love," said Pa, winking and throwing her a kiss.

It was a dreary day, not raining yet, but gray and threatening. We walked to the corner and looked back. Two heads were pressed against our front-room window, one small, one larger. Pa raised his hand and threw another kiss, then we turned up 107th.

The city was quiet. The pushcarts weren't even out yet, and a cop was just making his way up the street, rousting the sleeping bums out of doorways and alleys.

The window in Mr. Weissman's store was shiny and new again like nothing had ever happened. Pa walked by without a sideways glance.

Saying I'm sorry to Pa has always been hard for me. It's a lot easier with Ma somehow. With Pa the words just seem to stick in my throat. The business of last night was still unfinished between us, though, and I couldn't let him leave that way.

"Pa?" I said, my voice cracking a little as I hurried to keep up with him.

Pa didn't answer. His mind seemed somewhere else.

"Pa," I said again, a little louder.

"Huh? Oh, aye, Danny, what is it, lad?"

"I . . . uh . . . I'm real sorry about last night."

Pa nodded and his brows came together. "I know ya are, Danny, but promise me you'll steer clear o' them Sullivan boys while I'm gone."

"What do you mean, Pa?" I asked, pretending I didn't know what he was talking about.

"Enough with the games, Danny," said Pa. "We both know what I'm talkin' about. I'll be countin' on you to look after things while I'm gone. It's a man's job, and I need to know I can trust you with it."

My chest swelled up some at that. "Don't you worry," I told him. "I'll take care of everything. I'll make you real proud of me. I promise."

Pa smiled and clapped me on the back.

"Sure an' I know you will, lad."

We reached Fifth Avenue and Pa stopped. "You'd better get back now, Danny. See if you can pick up a few cents fer your ma before school."

I looked down at the sidewalk. It seemed like the day was suddenly growing darker.

"How long do you think it'll be, Pa?" I asked.

"Whatever it takes. I won't come home without a job."

I looked up. "You'll be coming home for Thanksgiving, at least?"

"I'll try my best," was all he said.

"Where will you go?"

"Don't know that either. I'll just be walkin' and askin', followin' up leads 'til I find somethin'. Might catch a train here and there if need be."

"Be careful, Pa."

"Don't you worry 'bout me, Danny."

Pa grabbed me around the shoulders and pulled me to his chest. I clung to him desperately for that moment, fighting back tears. I wanted to cry like a baby and beg him not to go, but I knew I had to put such thoughts behind me now. When he let me go I sniffed back the tears and stood tall and straight.

"Take care of our girls, Danny," he said.

"I will, Pa."

"Good-bye, lad."

"Good-bye, Pa."

He turned and walked up Fifth and I watched him until he crossed over and disappeared from view, heading west on 110th.

A big raindrop spattered down and made a dark spot on the sidewalk, then another, and another.

Oh, Pa, I thought. *You didn't even take an umbrella.*

EIGHT

Most days I don't mind shining shoes in the morning. I like to see the city waking up, the milk wagon making its rounds, the merchants opening their stores and sweeping their sidewalks, the horses coming through the tunnels from the stables on the other side, pulling the fruit and vegetable wagons. I was in a play at school last year, and that's what it reminds me of, being backstage before the curtain goes up.

Today, though, everything seemed dark and lonely. The rain was cold, and a wind came up and drove it into my face like icy needles. It was too wet to set up at my usual spot near Ike's newsstand, so I ducked inside the nearest subway entrance and set up there.

"Shoeshine, mister? Shoeshine?" I called out as the men began to filter in. Most of them ignored me, shuffling by with their heads tucked down inside their collars. Finally, one of them turned aside.

"How much?" he asked.

"Five cents," I told him.

He shook his head and started to walk away.

"Three cents?" I said hurriedly.

He paused and seemed to mull it over and over, like it was the biggest decision of his life. "How about two cents?" he offered.

I shrugged. "Okay."

The man put his foot up on the box and I did the best I could. The shoe was so worn it was hard to bring up a shine. Then he put the other foot up. I stared at it.

"Hey, mister," I said. "Do you know you got two different color shoes on?"

The man told me to shush and looked around sharply like he was embarrassed that someone might have heard.

"Of course I know it," he grumbled under his breath. "Just put some black polish on the brown one and try to make it look like the other. I got a job interview downtown."

"Yes, sir," I said. I gobbed black polish all over the shoe and rubbed it in as hard as I could. It worked pretty good. As long as the guy didn't cross his legs under anybody's nose, I guessed he might get away with it. It really wasn't such a big deal anyway. You see men wearing all kinds of mixed-up things these days—jackets that don't match their pants, suits that are too big or too small, patches all over everything.

"Thanks," he told me, handing me my two cents.

I nodded. "Good luck with your interview."

51

"Thanks. I'll need it. I gotta beat out about a hundred other guys."

"Whew," I said. "What's the job?"

"Shoe salesman."

I laughed. "Tell 'em you'll be your own first customer," I said.

He laughed, too. "Not bad, kid," he said. "I just might."

He hurried off and I watched the door for some other likely customers. At last a couple of spiffy-looking drugstore cowboys walked in, all decked out in their raccoon coats and slouch hats.

"Shoeshine, fellas?" I called out. "Regular five cents, on sale—two for a dime."

They looked at each other and laughed and started to walk over when suddenly I heard a shout.

"Hey you, kid!"

A rough-looking character was coming through the doors. He had a shoeshine box slung over his shoulder.

"What are you doing here? This is my territory. Get lost!"

I wasn't about to argue with someone twice my size and as old as my father. Besides, it was almost time for school anyway. I picked up my stuff and made a beeline for the door.

"I see you around here again, I'll break your legs," the tough shouted after me.

Jeez, I thought, *shining shoes is getting to be dangerous.*

Mama had my books all ready for me when I got

home. She frowned when she saw my wet hat and coat.

"Rainin' hard?" she asked.

"Yeah. Windy, too."

A shadow darkened her eyes.

"Don't worry, Mama," I said, "he won't melt."

She looked at me and smiled a little.

"No, I s'pose not."

"He'll be back real soon," I said, trying to make myself believe it, as well as her.

She nodded and gave me a kiss on the forehead. "Sure an' he will. Off with you now."

I hurried out the door and down the stairs. Mickey Crowley was waiting for me in the front hall. Mickey is fourteen and a head taller than me, but we're both in the same grade 'cause Mickey started school a year late.

"Hi, Danny," he called, looking over my shoulder back up the stairs.

I grinned at him. "Didn't she come down yet?"

Mickey turned red. "Who?"

"Kitty Riley. I know that's who you're looking for."

Mickey gave me a swat on the arm. "Aw, g'wan," he said, "just 'cause you're stuck on Maggie."

"Maggie?" I laughed. "You're full of applesauce, Mickey. Maggie's just like one of the guys."

There was a clamoring overhead and the Rileys came scrambling down the stairs, all except for Dotty and Marion. They're still too little to go to school. Johnny, Alice, Winnie, Florence, and Agnes are still in grammar school, but Kitty and Maggie, who are twins and the same age as me, go to the girls' junior high up on 111th. Kitty and Maggie are real twins— the kind that look alike, not the other kind, like Frank and Harry Sullivan. When they were little I used to mix them up a lot, but Maggie's taller now, and a little bit prettier, I think. Johnny's the only boy, poor kid. He'll be lucky if he doesn't turn out to be a sissy, living with eight sisters.

Kitty hung back a little when she saw us and gave Mickey a shy smile, but Maggie, as usual, came charging right over.

"Hey, Danny," she shouted. "What'd you do yesterday?"

"What do you mean, what did I do?"

"What did Finnegan nab you for?"

"None of your business."

"Aw c'mon, don't be like that."

I could see she was going to needle me until she got an answer, so I figured I might as well get it over with.

"Well, it wasn't my fault, but somehow a window got broken over at Weissman's and the penny jar got stolen."

Maggie's eyes narrowed. "That's lousy," she snapped. "I had a guess in on those pennies."

"So did I," I snapped. "I told you it wasn't my fault."

Maggie looked skeptical. "What'd your pa do?" she asked.

"He fixed it."

"I mean what'd he do to you?"

"Nothing."

"No kidding?" She sounded disappointed. "He didn't beat you or anything?"

"Nope."

Maggie shook her head like that was the strangest thing she'd ever heard. "Oh well," she said, "gotta go." She grabbed Kitty's hand and pulled her past Mickey.

We followed them out onto the stoop. "You little ones take the umbrella," Maggie told her sisters and brother. "Agnes, you hold it 'cause you're the tallest."

Ten-year-old Agnes took the umbrella and the others huddled around her like a bunch of baby chicks.

"Would you guys walk them through the tunnel?" Maggie asked us. "You know how it is on a rainy day."

She was talking about the 106th Street tunnel that the kids had to go through to get to school. All the tunnels that run under the train tracks over to the other side of Park Avenue are usually full of bums trying to stay dry on a day like today. It was out of our way to go through the tunnel and I was about to say so, when Mickey piped right up and said "Sure!" like she'd offered him a free licorice whip or something. Lately I can't figure him out.

Maggie told him thanks and gave him a big smile. Then she and Kitty opened a couple of sheets of newspaper over their heads and headed off up the avenue. Mickey and I watched them struggling against the wind, their skirts whipping around their knees. Mickey nudged me in the ribs.

"None of the guys I know has gams like that," he said.

I grabbed his cap off his head and swatted him with it, then I tossed it all the way across the gutter. It hit the trestle wall on the other side and slid down into a puddle.

"Hey!" he shouted, but I took off before he could grab me.

"Don't forget to walk the kids through the tunnel," I shouted over my shoulder.

NINE

I didn't have to wait long to get my hands on the Sullivan boys. Before I knew it they had their hands on me. When I got to school they were waiting right inside the front door. They each grabbed an arm and the next thing I knew I was pinned up against the wall.

"Did you rat?" Harry asked me in a hoarse whisper.

"Yeah, did you?" repeated Frank, pulling out the front of my jacket.

"Shut up, stupid, I can handle this," Harry told his brother. Then he turned back to me. "Did you?" he asked again.

"Look," I said. "Do you think you'd be standing here if I'da ratted?"

"What d'ya mean?" asked Harry.

The Sullivans aren't known for the size of their brains.

"I mean, if I'da ratted, the cops would've come after you by now, don't you think?"

Harry and Frank looked at each other and considered this for a minute. Meanwhile Mickey came in, saw what was going on, gave me a smirk, and walked right by.

Harry finally finished his considering, nodded to Frank, and they let me go. Then it was my turn. I grabbed ahold of Harry's thumb and twisted it back.

It was a trick Pa had taught me. "You're not gonna be big, Danny," he had said, "so you have to be smart and you have to be quick." I remember feeling bad when he said that, like it was my fault I took after Ma instead of him. I made up my mind right then and there to be so quick and so smart that he'd be proud of me just the same.

I had Harry down on his knees begging for mercy, but still I twisted harder.

"I had to take the rap for you," I told him, "and you're gonna pay for it, you hear? And what's more, I figure that money you stole was practically mine—"

"Hey! Hey! What's going on here?"

It was Mr. Whitelaw, the vice principal. He's got a knack for always showing up at the wrong times. I let go of Harry and he got to his feet, rubbing his thumb. He kicked his brother in the leg.

"Why didn't you help me, you idiot?" he growled.

Frank grabbed his leg and whimpered. "You said you could handle it."

"Aw, shut up," said Harry, then he looked at me. "I'll get you back for this, Garvey."

"All right, all right, that's enough out of you two," said Mr. Whitelaw. He sent us off in opposite directions.

"Thanks for all your help," I whispered to Mickey as I slid into the seat in front of him in English class.

"You looked like you were holding your own," he answered.

"Yeah, sure. I'll remember to return the favor next time you're in a jam."

Mr. Proctor came in and told us to open to chapter eight of *Tom Sawyer*. Then he called on Tony Maretti to read aloud. I tried to pay attention, but my mind kept drifting away. I finished the whole book a couple of days after he gave it to us anyway. I don't know why we can't just get a new book every time we finish reading one. It's so boring to go chapter by chapter and then to have to pick it all apart and say what the book *means* to you. The thing is, the teachers don't really give a hoot what the book means to you. All they care about is what it means to *them*.

Take *Black Beauty* for instance. *Black Beauty* is my all-time favorite book, but not because of any message about social injustice like Mr. Proctor tried to tell us. *Black Beauty* is my all-time favorite book because of Ned.

Ned is the horse that pulls the ice wagon, and for years Ned and I didn't understand each other. Every time the ice wagon came, while the ice man was in making deliveries and the other kids were all jumping in and out of the wagon and grabbing chunks of ice, I would talk to Ned. I would run my hand along his poor old saggy back and wonder if it was ever straight and strong, and I would comb his tangled mane with my fingers. Sometimes, if Ma had a spare carrot or a bit of apple, I would feed it to him. And always he would look at me with his great big sad eyes. I knew he had a story to tell, but he couldn't make me understand. Then I read *Black Beauty,* and I understood about Ned. That's what I wrote in my composition, and I got a C minus.

"Hey, Dan."

It was Mickey, leaning close to my shoulder.

"Yeah?"

"Luther's absent."

I looked across the aisle at the empty chair where Luther usually sat. I nodded. "His family got evicted yesterday."

"No kidding," whispered Mickey. "I know that. I live in his building—"

"Master Garvey?"

"Uh . . . yes sir?"

"Would you tell us in your own words what Mark Twain meant by that passage?"

"Uh . . ."

TEN

Staying after school to write one hundred times "I will pay attention in class" made me late for my first day at Mr. Weissman's store. He didn't say anything about it when I came in. He just took Pa's watch out, held it up, and looked at it fondly, then dropped it back into his vest pocket.

"Sorry I'm late, Mr. Weissman. Something came up at school. It won't happen again."

"Did you know it would happen today?"

"No sir."

"Then you don't know it won't happen again. You'll stay fifteen minutes overtime. Put your apron on."

"Yes sir."

"This is the cash register, I'm sure you know— but I'm going to teach you something new. I'm going to teach you to put money *in* instead of stealing it *out*."

"Mr. Weissman, I told you, I'm not a thief."

"I know, I know. An angel you are. So you say. We'll see." He patted his vest pocket.

Mr. Weissman showed me how to work the register. It was kind of fun, actually.

"And I know exactly how much is in there, so don't get any ideas."

"Yes sir," I mumbled, tired of arguing.

"Over here is the milk jug," Mr. Weissman went on. "When a customer brings his can in, you fill it to the neck line, no more, no less. The same with the flour. Put the sack on the scale and weigh out just what the customer asks for, no more, no less. And as for the penny candy . . ."

"I know, I know," I told him, "just what they ask for, no more, no less."

"Good," said Mr. Weissman. "Now this is the ledger." He pulled a heavy black book from under the counter. "Here I keep the accounts of all my regular customers. If someone wants credit, you look up the name in the book and write down how much. If the name isn't in the book—no credit!"

Mr. Weissman shouted this at me, like I was the one asking for credit.

"You understand?"

"Yes sir."

"Good. Now open that box on the floor and stack the cans in that empty spot up there on the shelf."

"Do I get to climb the ladder?" I asked. The ladders that grocers slide back and forth and climb up and down on always looked like fun to me.

"What do you think, you throw them up there? Of course you climb the ladder."

"Wow! Keen!" I said.

Mr. Weissman rolled his eyes up to the ceiling and shook his head.

While I was up on the ladder a lady came in. She was well dressed for the neighborhood, with a big fur collar and a fancy black velvet hat, but she had a sour expression and a little pinched mouth that made her look like she'd enjoy sucking lemons. She held a paper sack out at arm's length like it was a dead rat.

"Mr. Weissman!" she said, in a drill sergeant kind of voice. "This flour has a *worm* in it."

"Good afternoon, Miss Perkins," said Mr. Weissman. "It's a pleasure to see you, too."

I stared at the woman. Her name sounded familiar, but I couldn't place her face. She didn't react to Mr. Weissman's greeting. She just sniffed loudly and shook the sack at him. Mr. Weissman took it from her and looked inside.

"Ah, and a fine meaty fellow he is, too. How good of you to call him to my attention." Mr. Weissman looked up at Miss Perkins. His bushy eyebrows came together and he pulled at his beard. "For such a good customer," he said, "a special deal. Keep the flour *and* the worm—no extra charge."

Miss Perkins's mouth fell open and I nearly slipped

off the ladder, trying not to laugh. In an instant, though, she snapped it shut again and narrowed her eyes.

"Mr. Weissman," she warned, "*don't* toy with me."

Mr. Weissman chuckled. "I can assure you, Miss Perkins," he told her, "nothing is further from my mind."

Miss Perkins stuck her chin forward and crossed her arms over her chest. "I want a new sack of flour," she said, "and I want it *now.*"

Mr. Weissman shrugged. "Some people you can't please," he said, then he looked up at me. "Danny, come down here and weigh out a pound of flour for Miss Perkins."

"Yes sir."

I measured out the flour until it weighed exactly a pound, no more, no less. I handed the bag to the lady and suddenly I remembered where I'd heard her name before. Miss Perkins used to be Maggie's teacher over at the annex a couple of years ago. Poor Maggie! Miss Perkins snatched the bag from my hand without a word of thanks and marched out the door.

I looked after her. "No wonder they call her the storm trooper," I said.

Mr. Weissman looked at me and arched an eyebrow. "What's that you say?"

"The girls over at the annex where she teaches, they call her the storm trooper."

I thought for a minute that I saw a smile lurking around the corners of Mr. Weissman's mouth, but a second later it was gone.

"Here," he said, handing me the sack in his hand. "Pick out the worm and put the flour back in the bin."

"Back in the bin?"

"Yes, back in the bin." Mr. Weissman looked up and started talking to the ceiling. "Such a fuss over a little worm," he said. "In my whole life I should get so much attention."

Well, I'm not too fond of worms, but I did as Mr. Weissman said.

"What do you want me to with it?" I asked when I'd fished the thing out.

"Eat it. You could use the meat."

I nearly gagged.

"What's the matter? You don't like raw meat? Take it home then. Tell your mother to make a stew. I have to get something in the back. Try not to rob me blind while I'm gone."

I was still standing there with my stomach churning and the worm in my hand when the bell on the door dinged and Mrs. White walked in. She seemed embarrassed to see me.

"Oh, hello, Danny," she said. "What are you doing behind the counter?"

"I'm . . . sort of helping out for a while, ma'am."

"Isn't that nice. What a good boy to be such a help to your family in these hard times."

"Yes ma'am," I said, feeling pretty guilty.

"What's that you're holding there?"

"Oh, uh, nothing," I dropped the mealworm into my apron pocket. "Can I help you with something?"

Mrs. White blushed and looked down at the purse she held in her two hands.

"Well, as you know we are . . . moving, and we have made a little money selling off some of our things, so I have come to settle our account."

"Yes ma'am," I said, pulling the book from under the counter. "Any idea where you'll be moving to?"

Mrs. White blushed again. "We . . . uh, haven't decided yet."

"Oh. Well, tell Luther to drop me a postcard and let me know where you are once you're settled."

"I'll do that, Danny, thank you."

I opened the book to the *W*'s and flipped through the accounts until I came to White. "Here it is," I said, running my hand down the column of figures. "That'll be—"

The book was suddenly jerked from my hands, and I turned to find Mr. Weissman standing beside me.

"I'll take care of this, Danny," he said. "You get back to those cans." He turned and smiled at Mrs. White. "How are you today, Mrs. White?" he asked her.

She gave him small smile in return. "Well enough, thank you, Mr. Weissman."

"And the children?"

"Fine, also."

"Good. Good. I'm sorry to hear you'll be leaving us."

"I'm sorry, too, Mr. Weissman." She dropped her eyes. "About the bill, please."

"Yes, of course. Let me see now." Mr. Weissman ran his finger down the page. "That'll be seven dollars and twenty-two cents."

I stopped stacking cans and stared at him. I had just read that account. It said thirty-three dollars and eighty-seven cents.

"Uh . . . oh," stammered Mrs. White. "There must be some mistake. I'm sure it's much higher than that."

Mr. Weissman looked at the book again. "No," he said, "no mistake."

"But surely . . ."

"Surely you don't accuse me of not knowing my business?"

"Why, no, of course not. . . ."

"Good, then you have cash?"

"Oh, yes." Mrs. White fumbled in her purse and counted out seven one-dollar bills and some change. "And . . . uh, I'll be needing a few groceries as well," she added.

Mr. Weissman got the items she asked for and put them in a sack. Mrs. White opened her purse again, but Mr. Weissman waved her hand away.

"A farewell gift," he said, pushing the sack across the counter.

"Oh no, I couldn't," said Mrs. White, putting her money down.

Mr. Weissman picked up the bills and pushed them back into her hand. "I always give my customers a going-away gift," he said gruffly. "Good business. Tell your friends." He grabbed a handful of licorice whips and threw them into the bag. "For the children," he added.

Mrs. White finally gave in and accepted the sack.

"Bless you, Mr. Weissman," she said quietly.

Mr. Weissman smiled. "A blessing I can always use," he said.

As soon as the door closed behind Mrs. White, I jumped down from the ladder. "Mr. Weissman," I said, "I saw that account. I thought it said . . ."

With a loud snap Mr. Weissman tore the page from the book and crumpled it into a ball.

"I didn't ask you what you think," he said. "I asked you to stack cans. Now get back to work."

ELEVEN

Friday, October 21, 1932

I decided today to give up stealing forever.

Being awful hungry, I had sneaked a few peanuts out of the bin at the store, figuring Mr. Weissman would never miss a handful. I had put them into my apron pocket and was tossing one into my mouth every time Mr. Weissman turned his back, when I bit into one that crackled strangely. I tasted something kind of gooey and sour, and I spit it into my hand.

"Oh no-o-o-o," I moaned.

"What? What's the matter?" asked Mr. Weissman.

"Miss Perkins's worm," I groaned, my stomach flipping over. "I just ate it."

Mr. Weissman started to laugh, then he made a stern face and pointed to the ceiling. "He got you," he said.

I looked up. All I could see was a spider, who

admittedly might not be too crazy about me horning in on his bug supply, but I didn't really see how he could have "gotten me."

"Who?" I asked.

"Him," said Mr. Weissman, pointing to the ceiling again.

Then I figured out that me meant the *big* Him.

"He got you," said Mr. Weissman, "for stealing peanuts."

I felt myself blushing. "You knew?" I said quietly.

"Of course I knew. I have eyes in the back of my head. You don't see them, but they're there."

"I'm sorry, Mr. Weissman. Really I am. I'll work an extra day to pay for them."

Mr. Weissman waved my words away. "A handful of peanuts I can afford," he said. "Only next time *ask,* don't steal."

I was really mad at myself, not only because I'd gone back on my word to Pa, but because I've come to like crotchety old Mr. Weissman with his gruff ways and his heart of gold. I want him to like me, too.

It hasn't taken me long to figure out why the Weissmans live as poor as they do. It's not for lack of business. The little bell over the door dings all day long. The trouble is, the bell in the cash register hardly ever dings at all. Everybody just keeps saying, "Put it on my bill," and the numbers in the black book get bigger and bigger, while Mr. Weissman's wallet gets thinner and thinner.

Working in the store has been causing a problem for me, too—one I hadn't figured on. See, as soon as word got out that I was working there, all my friends started showing up, thinking I'd let them get away without paying. It was really rough, especially in the beginning, before I figured out about Mr. Weissman; because here I was working for this supposedly rich old guy, and here were all my friends, just looking for a little something to fill their bellies, and I'm stuck in the middle. If I give the stuff away and get caught I disappoint Pa, and Mr. Weissman gets to keep the watch. If I don't give the stuff away, my friends think I'm a rat fink.

So that's how I got to be a rat fink.

And that's not the worst of my problems. Who showed up at the store this afternoon but the Sullivan boys, which took some nerve, I thought. But then the Sullivan boys are about as long on nerve as they are short on brain.

Mr. Weissman was busy with a customer when they came in.

"Well, look who's here," said Harry. "What are you doing working here, Danny boy?"

"You know very well what I'm doing here," I said under my breath so Mr. Weissman wouldn't hear.

"Helping out, huh?" Harry went on. "Well, that's real nice. Ain't that nice, Frank?"

"Nice," said Frank.

I scowled. "What can I do for you?" I asked.

"Gee, polite, too," said Harry. "You're just so

polite I think you ought to get a raise. Don't you think he ought to get a raise, Frank?"

"Shut up, Harry," I said.

"Uh-oh, uh-oh, now is that any way to talk to a customer?"

"You ain't no customer, Harry."

"Now see here, you're wrong," said Harry. "I got a dime right here says I am."

Mr. Weissman's customer had left and he was standing there watching us.

"Well then, what can I do for you?" I asked again.

"Our ma wants a loaf of bread and three cents' worth of sugar," said Harry.

"Danny," Mr. Weissman interrupted, "you can handle this. I'll be in the back."

I couldn't believe my ears. Of all times to leave me alone. He knew darn well the Sullivan boys meant trouble.

I got the bread and weighed out the sugar. I handed the bag to Harry.

"That'll be ten cents," I said.

Harry dropped the dime back into his pocket.

"And you can kiss my butt," he said.

I looked toward the back room.

"Aw, you gonna call mommy?" said Harry in a whiny voice. "Look at that, Frank, he's gonna call mommy."

"Awwww," said Frank.

I stared at them. "Give me the money, Harry."

"Put it on my bill," he said. "Let's go, Frank."

"You don't have credit here, Harry," I told him, "and you know it."

Harry just shrugged and kept on walking. I had to do something quick. I wasn't about to let Mr. Weissman think I'd let them get away without paying. I jumped the counter, cut in front of them, and blocked the door.

"Give me the dime, Harry," I said again.

"Gee," said Harry, "there's something in the way. I guess we better move it, Frank."

"Guess so," said Frank.

They both lunged forward and grabbed me, one under each arm, and hoisted me up. I kicked my legs out and twisted them around one each of theirs, and the three of us went down with a crash.

"Hey, hey!" yelled Mr. Weissman, rushing out of the back room. "What is this, what is this?"

"Nothing, sir," I said, getting up and brushing myself off. "Harry and Frank were just paying for their groceries, weren't you, fellas?"

Harry glared at me. He took the dime out and slapped it into my open hand. I picked up their bag from where it had landed under the three of us.

"Sorry about your bread," I said. "Maybe your ma can make a pudding."

Harry grabbed the bag out of my hand, swore under his breath, and left with Frank tagging after.

"Thank you. Come again," I shouted after them. Mr. Weissman smiled.

"What'd you leave me alone for?" I asked. "You know those two are trouble."

Mr. Weissman just shrugged and stroked his beard. Then something dawned on me.

"You were testing me, weren't you?" I said.

The bell dinged and a customer walked in.

"Good afternoon, Mrs. Salinas," said Mr. Weissman, ignoring my question. "How can we help you today?"

TWELVE

It was dusk when I walked home from the store. Normally I keep a pretty sharp eye out, but being that tonight was Friday, my mind was full of all the swell things I was planning for tomorrow. I was trying to figure out how I could cram the most good stuff into one day. I was almost home, when suddenly I was grabbed from behind. My arms were pinned in back of me, and Harry Sullivan's face appeared in front of me just long enough for him to land a punch in my gut that knocked the wind out of me. While I was helpless like that, all doubled over, sucking and gulping for air, Harry and Frank dragged me back into an alley and pinned me up against the wall, smashing my face against the bricks.

"Look what we got here," said Harry. "Gee, if it ain't the neighborhood rat fink." He gave my head a rough shove and my face scraped painfully along the wall.

"What do you want, Harry?" I asked when I could breathe again.

"What do we want?" Harry's face appeared in front of mine and he smiled a hateful smile. "Let's start with an 'I'm sorry.' " He twisted my arm behind me.

Use your head when you're in trouble, Pa always said. *There's a time to be tough and a time to be smart.* This was a time to be smart.

"Sorry," I mumbled.

"Louder," shouted Harry, twisting harder.

"Sorry," I shouted.

"I don't think he sounds sorry enough, do you, Frank?"

"Nah," said Frank.

"I think he needs to be taught a lesson," said Harry. "Get down on your knees, fink."

He shoved me down, my face scraping against the wall again. The skin was raw now and the wet feel of the bricks told me I was bleeding.

Harry and Frank leaned over me, and I heard the unmistakable sound of a knife blade sliding open and snapping into place. My insides turned to ice and every hair on my body stood up. I opened my mouth to scream, but no sound came out. Then, all of a sudden, they let me go and stepped back. I turned my head cautiously, afraid of what might happen next. What I saw made my breath come out in a whoosh of relief. It wasn't Harry and Frank who had the

76

knife, but Mickey Crowley, who stood spread-legged, blocking the entrance to the alley.

"Mickey," I said, "am I glad to see you."

Harry and Frank glared at him. "This ain't none of your affair, Crowley," said Harry. "Why don't you just butt out?"

"I wouldn't expect you to know this, Harry," said Mickey, "never having had any yourself. But Danny's a friend of mine, and friends stick together."

Mickey moved forward, raising the knife, and Harry and Frank retreated farther back into the alley. Mickey clapped a hand on my shoulder.

"You okay?"

I got shakily to my feet. "Yeah, fine."

Mickey put a hand under my chin and turned my face toward the light from the street.

"Now, would you look at that," he said. "That ain't nice. That ain't nice at all. I think I'm gonna have to spill some Sullivan blood to make up for it."

Harry and Frank shrank back into the shadows. Frank started to whimper and Harry socked him in the stomach. "Shut up," he whispered hoarsely. "Shut up or I'll kill you myself." *Poor Frank,* I thought, *born two minutes after his brother and living in his shadow ever since.*

"Let 'em go," I told Mickey.

"Oh, I'll let 'em go. I just want to see them bleed a little first."

"Let 'em go now, Mick."

Mickey looked at me and frowned. "You're no

fun at all, you know that?" he said, but he lowered the knife and stepped aside. "Go on, get out of here," he told Frank and Harry. "But if I was you I'd stick close to home from now on."

Frank ran like a scared rabbit, but Harry walked by slow and deliberate. The guy has guts, I have to give him that. When he got to the entrance of the alley, he turned back and stared at us. "Nobody tells Harry Sullivan where he can and can't go," he said. "I'll be back." Then he disappeared.

Me and Mickey burst out laughing. I grabbed the knife out of his hand.

"Where the heck did you get this?" I asked.

"Pa took it off some guys last night."

Mickey's father is a night watchman.

"Yeah?" I said. "Well, he'll use it to skin you alive if he finds out you've got it."

"Aw, he won't know. I'll put it back in his drawer before he gets home. Came in handy, though, didn't it?"

I started laughing again. "I'm gonna spill me some Sullivan blood," I mimicked. "You been watching too many movies, Mickey. Poor Frank probably peed his pants."

"Ah, he deserves it."

"Nah, Frank ain't bad. He just never learned to think, that's all. Harry's been telling him what to do all his life. Harry probably kicked him in the gut the minute he was born and said, 'Cry, stupid.' "

Mickey laughed. "Yeah, you're probably right." He folded the knife and put it away and we started walking home. He took another look at my face under the streetlamp.

"Ain't bad," he said. "Just tore up some. You were too pretty anyway."

I gave him a kick.

"Hey listen," he said. "I been waitin' for you. I wanted to talk to you about something."

"Yeah? What?"

"Well . . . uh . . ." Mickey suddenly seemed to lose his voice.

"What?" I said again.

"Well . . . what do you say we take Kitty and Maggie to the movies tomorrow?"

I stopped and stared at him. "*Take* them to the movies? What do you mean, *take* them to the movies?"

"You know, like on a date."

"A date! You mean us pay?"

"Yeah. What's wrong with that?"

"Are you nuts? You *must* be nuts."

"Why? Would you tell me that? Why am I nuts?"

"Because I'm not paying for any girl to go see no movie. If they want to see a movie they can pay their own way, just like the rest of us."

"You know they ain't got no money with all them kids and the way their pa is."

"Yeah, well that's not my problem. In case you haven't noticed, my name ain't Rockefeller, either."

"Look, Danny, I'll pay for all of us."

"Oh sure. What'd you do, rob a bank?"

"Naw, I just got it, that's all."

I stared at him. "You didn't steal it, did you? I promised my pa I wouldn't have nothin' more to do with stealing."

"No, I didn't steal it. If you have to know, my grandmother gave me a dollar when she came to visit last weekend."

"A whole dollar?"

"Yeah, a whole dollar."

"Whew! I didn't know you had rich relatives, Mickey. I'm impressed."

"Aw, shut up. Do you wanna go or not?"

"I don't know. I still think you're crazy. Do you know what you can buy with a dollar? You could go to the movies ten times, or you could buy twenty Baby Ruths, or fifty Hooton Bars, or . . ."

"Will you shut up? I think I know what I can buy."

"Then why don't you?"

" 'Cause I'm not a kid anymore."

"Oh, whoa. . . . So what are you, a man?"

"More of a man than you'll ever be."

"Aaagh!" I grabbed my throat, choking and sputtering like I was gonna die laughing.

Mickey socked me in the shoulder. "Grow up, will you?" he said. "Are you going or not?"

"No way."

"Okay," said Mickey. "I was hoping I wouldn't have to bring this up, but the way I see it, you owe me one."

I stopped laughing. He had me there.

"All right then," I said. "Have it your way. But

I'll tell you something. They're never gonna say yes. Maggie Riley will fall down laughing when we ask her."

Mickey grinned. "We'll see," he said. "We'll just see."

We had reached my stoop by then. "See you in the morning," I said.

"Wait a minute," said Mickey. "When are we gonna ask them?"

I turned to look at him. "Not now, you thick mick. Bad enough I gotta do it in the first place. I'm sure not gonna do it with a face full of blood."

Mickey scowled. "Okay," he said, "in the morning then, but don't get any ideas about chickening out." He shoved his hands into his pockets and walked away.

Maggie and Kitty were right inside the front door when I walked in. They were scrubbing the floors like they usually do on Friday nights. My face got all hot when I saw them.

"Well, well," said Maggie, "if it isn't the rat fink."

"Knock it off, Maggie," I told her. "You don't know how it is."

"Oh yeah? Why don't you tell me then?"

"Some other time."

"Hey. What happened to your face?"

"I fell."

"Yeah, I bet. Watch your dirty feet, huh? We just scrubbed those stairs. Why don't you take your shoes off?"

"Ah, go cook a radish." I bounded up the stairs

two at a time and looked back down when I got to the landing. Maggie and Kitty had already forgotten about me and were back to their usual gabbing and giggling. They sure beat that Tom Sawyer fella for making work look like fun.

I watched them for a minute. Mickey was right. Maggie sure doesn't look like one of the guys anymore. I sighed. Why do things have to change? It makes life so complicated.

THIRTEEN

Mama wasn't ironing when I walked in. All the linens were neatly folded and stacked, ready for me to deliver in the morning. Maureen was playing in the tub, 'and Mama was sitting at the table, writing a letter.

"Who're you writing to?" I asked her.

"Yer daddy," she said, without looking up.

"You've heard from him already!"

"No," said Mama, "but I'm writin' just the same."

"Where you gonna send it?"

"Wherever he is, if he stays put long enough. If not, I'll just be savin' it 'til he's home again."

That didn't make a lot of sense to me.

"What do you want to do that for?" I asked.

"Because I don't want him to be missin' anything while he's gone. Besides, it gives me comfort, Danny, to talk with him this way."

I nodded. "Tell him 'hi' for me," I said.

Mama smiled and looked up.

"Oh, Mother o' God," she said, "what've ya done to yer face?"

"It's nothing, Ma. Just a few scratches is all."

She got up out of her chair and came over and turned my face to the light.

"Aw, Danny," she said, "what happened?"

"Nothin', Ma. I fell, that's all."

"On yer face?"

"Yeah, on my face."

"Give me yer hands."

Reluctantly I put my hands into hers. She turned them over and looked at the palms.

"It's full of the blarney you are," she said, then she sighed. "Are you gonna tell me the truth now?"

I stared at the floor.

Mama dropped my hands and shook her head angrily.

"Stubborn," she said, "stubborn like a mule. It's a mold of yer father you are."

I grinned at her. "I guess I could do worse then, huh?"

Mama snorted. "Aye, and I can see you've got his smooth Garvey tongue as well. Come over here then and see if you can talk yer way out of *this*." She pushed the curtains under the sink aside and pulled out a brown bottle.

"Oh no, Ma, not the peroxide," I said. "Not your life." I hopped around her and went over to the tub and kissed Maureen on the top of her damp little head.

"Da," she said, holding her soppy wet arms up to me. I was about to grab her towel when I felt Ma's firm grip on my ear.

"Ouch, Ma. Cut that out."

"Never you mind," she said, steering me over to the sink.

"C'mon, Ma. Please?"

"Close yer eyes and tilt yer head to the side."

"But . . ."

There was another sharp tug on my ear.

"All right, all right." I gritted my teeth and waited. "Yee-ouch!" The medicine felt like a wire brush dragging across my raw skin. I pulled away, but Ma pulled me right back and went at it again.

"Sweet Jesus, Ma," I shouted. "Talk about being killed by the cure!"

"There," she said finally, handing me a towel. "That'll give ya something to think about next time yer tempted to go brawlin'. And don't let me catch ya takin' our Lord's name in vain again, or I'll wash out yer mouth as well."

She would, too. Ma may be little, but she's feisty. Maureen was staring at us with her mouth hanging open and her eyes bugged out. I guess she must've thought Ma was killing me or something. I took the towel and went over and scooped her out of the tub.

"Da's okay," I told her, "don't you worry." She was rosy red and steamy inside the towel. I rubbed her dry, tickling her as I did and making her giggle. I pinned up her diaper, then slipped her into the nightgown and booties Ma had laid out for her. She looked like a cherub with her pink cheeks and little damp ringlets. I flew her around in the air and made her giggle some more. I caught a glimpse of Ma as I spun around. All the anger was gone from her eyes.

"Aye," she said, nodding with a smile on her lips, "a mold of your father to be sure."

I laughed, embarrassed, and brought Maureen in for a landing on the kitchen table. "What's for supper?" I asked. "I'm starving."

Ma's smile faded. "It'll be oatmeal again, I'm afraid."

I felt bad for asking. Of course it was oatmeal again. Ma had hidden our last three dollars in the sack she'd packed for Pa, so we'd been living on oatmeal and evaporated milk for days.

"Hey, that's okay. I like oatmeal," I said as cheerfully as I could. "Besides, tomorrow's payday."

Ma gave me a sheepish look.

"Ya must think me daft, packin' the whole three dollars like that."

It made me angry, her thinking that way. "Of course I don't," I told her. "Do you think I could swallow my supper knowing Pa had none? I only wish we'd had more to give."

Ma nodded and set out the bowls. She took the pot from the back of the stove and scooped out the pasty goo. There was sugar at least, and the oatmeal was warm and thick enough to fill up the cave in my stomach—for a little while, anyway. We were just finishing up when I noticed the end of a rag mop swishing back and forth outside our window.

"Mrs. Mahoney wants you, Ma," I said.

Mrs. Mahoney is the widow who lives upstairs. The thump, thump, thump, of her wooden leg overhead is as much a part of our lives as the rumble of the elevated train across the street.

Mama went over, raised the window, and stuck her head out.

"Aye, Rose?" she yelled.

"Come up for a cuppa tea," Mrs. Mahoney yelled back.

Mama smiled. She looked at me. "Do ya think you could tuck Maureen in?" she asked.

"Sure, Ma. Go ahead."

"I'll just be a minute, Rose," Mama called out the window again.

Mrs. Mahoney's kitchen is the gathering spot for all the women in the building. It's supposed to be a secret that the "tea" she serves in real china cups is actually homemade wine. But us kids all know, and we giggle behind our hands when our mothers come back downstairs smiling a bit too widely.

Wine and beer are illegal to buy, because of Prohibition. That's why lots of folks make their own. I guess that's not illegal, as long as they don't try to sell it. Besides, the cops are too busy chasing after all the big-time gangsters and bootleggers to worry much about ordinary people like Mrs. Mahoney. Pa says there's an awful lot of hoodlums getting rich off Prohibition, and the sooner it ends the better.

Mama scurried around cleaning up the supper dishes, then she pulled off her apron and straightened the pins in her hair.

"Sure ya don't mind now?" she asked me.

"Not a bit, Ma."

"Don't be forgettin' yer bath then."

"Aw, Ma."

"Do as yer told now." She kissed Maureen goodnight and paused in the doorway. "I'll put the radio on for you," she said, flicking the knob. Kate Smith's voice filled the room. Ma stood still and listened, her gaze far away. When the song ended she shook her head in admiration. "Sure an' that girl can sing," she said.

"Not as good as you, Ma," I told her. "You could've been a singer on the radio."

Ma threw her head back and laughed—a laugh so full of music it sounded like someone running their hand down the keyboard of a piano.

"Aye," she said, "and I could've been the queen of England, too, if I'da married me the king."

I could still hear her laughing to herself as she climbed the stairs. I put the water on to boil for my bath while I tucked Maureen in, then I filled the tub.

I sure hate taking a bath. Not that I'm a slob or anything. It's just that our tub is right in the middle of the kitchen, and even though I pull the shades down and lock the door, I still feel naked to the world.

Once, a couple of years ago, Maggie walked right in while I was sitting there—nothing between her and me but a bar of soap. She never lets me forget it, either. I've grown up some since then, if you know what I mean. A bar of soap wouldn't be too much help anymore. We got a chain lock on the kitchen door now, but I still panic every time I hear footsteps in the hall.

I climbed in and went about my business as quickly as I could. "Amos 'n' Andy" came on the radio and had me laughin' in no time. They are the funniest guys. All of a sudden, in the middle of a laugh, this knock came on the door.

"Danny?" It was Maggie's voice. I sank down in the water.

"Danny? Want to come over and play Monopoly?"

I didn't answer. I wasn't about to let on that I was in the tub.

"Danny, I know you're in there. I heard you laughin'." Then there was a giggle. "Why aren't you answering?"

The next think I knew, I heard her key turning in the lock. The door opened a crack and then the chain stopped it. "D-a-n-n-y," came Maggie's sing-songy voice. "Are you in the tub?"

I swallowed hard and stayed as still as death. The tub was out of the line of view of the crack, but still, Maggie Riley's eyes were staring into the very room that I was stark naked in. I never realized before that you could sweat underwater.

FOURTEEN

Saturday, October 22, 1932

Saturday morning is usually slow shining shoes, but today was the worst. I stood out there next to Ike's newsstand for a solid hour and all I made was one lousy nickel. I think Ike must've felt sorry for me, 'cause just as I was packing up he asked me for a shine.

"Ah, you don't need one," I told him.

"Sure I do. Got a date with my girl tonight. Gotta look spiffy." He gave me a wink.

I didn't really believe him, but I wasn't about to argue too hard. After all, a nickel's a nickel, and they are gettin' harder and harder to come by.

I handed both nickels to Ma when I got home. "That's all I got," I apologized.

Ma looked at the two nickels, then handed them back to me. "You go to the movies," she said.

"I don't need 'em, Ma," I told her. "I'm already going to the movies. Mickey's payin'."

Ma looked at me strangely. "Why?" she asked.

"It's a long story. I'll tell you later. I gotta get going."

"Well, you take this anyway," said Ma, pressing the money into my hand. "Buy you and Mickey a Baby Ruth. You deserve it."

"No kidding?"

Mama grinned and tousled my hair. "No kidding. Now off to Miss Emily's, and don't dawdle on the way."

I carried the linens downstairs, loaded them into my wagon, and headed over to Miss Emily's Hotel for Young Women. Sadie let me in the back door. She's the cook—a big colored lady with cheeks that shine like polished mahogany and eyes full of laughter.

"Mawnin', child," she said, giving me a wide, warm smile. "How y'all doin' this day?"

"Just fine, Sadie," I told her. I don't know how she stays so cheerful, working for the likes of Miss Emily. Miss Emily is as bony and cold as Sadie is round and warm.

The kitchen smelled of good things to eat. Beyond the swinging doors I could hear the clink of silverware and the murmur of conversation. Sadie went to tell Miss Emily I was there. As I was bringing in the linens, a maid started carrying the finished plates out into the kitchen. I couldn't believe my eyes.

Some of them were hardly touched, still heaped with eggs, pancakes, biscuits, and thick slabs of ham. Just looking at them made my stomach growl and my mouth flood up with water.

Sadie bustled back in and caught me staring at the food.

"Ain't it a shame," she said, shaking her head. "These fine ladies always fussin' over their little bitty waistlines—eat like birds, the lot of 'em." Then she grinned and gave me a wink. "I keep tellin' 'em, a man likes a little flesh on a woman. Ain't that the truth?"

I felt myself blushing. "Yes, ma'am, I suppose so," I said. The next thing I knew, my eyes got pulled back to that food again. Jeez, that cave in my stomach was aching.

Sadie grabbed a big biscuit from one of the plates, split it open, spread it thick with butter, and loaded on two huge slabs of ham.

"Here," she said, holding it out to me. "Ain't no use lettin' good food go to waste."

My fingers itched to reach for it, but I held them still.

"I already had breakfast, thanks."

Sadie turned her head sideways and looked me up and down. "Lawd, child," she said, "don't look to me like you're in need of watchin' your weight." She pushed the biscuit into my hand.

I pushed it back. "Mama don't let me take charity," I said quietly.

"Charity! That what you think this is? That ain't what this is. This is soul savin'."

"Soul savin'?"

"Shore 'nuff. Ain't you ever heard that it's a sin to waste food?"

"Yes, ma'am."

"Well then. You'd just be savin' the souls of them fine ladies in there if you was to eat this up now, wouldn't you?"

I knew it was all a bunch of baloney, but I just couldn't hold out any longer. I took the biscuit and bit in. I thought for sure I'd died and gone to heaven. I'd never tasted anything so rich and good in my whole life. As hungry as I was, I chewed it slowly, pushing it around my mouth with my tongue, trying to get every last drop of flavor out before I swallowed it down.

Just then Miss Emily walked in. She glanced at me briefly, scowled, and looked away. She went over to Sadie and put a ten-dollar bill in her hand.

"I told you not to be giving handouts to these waifs," she said, not caring that I was standing right there. "It just makes them lazy and shiftless." Then she turned and marched out again without another glance in my direction.

There was hatred burning in Sadie's eyes as she handed me the money. "You never mind her," she said, but it was too late. The biscuit had turned as sour as throw-up in my mouth. I swallowed it with difficulty and put the rest down on the table. I reached into my pocket and touched the two nickels Ma had given me. I held them for a minute, just thinking about those Baby Ruths, but then in my mind I saw Miss Emily's scowling face and felt the sting of her words again. I pulled the nickels out and plunked them down next to the biscuit.

"Would you make sure Miss Emily gets these," I asked Sadie.

Her eyes met mine, and then a slow, approving smile spread across her face. She nodded and gave me a wink.

"I shore will, honey," she said softly. "I shore 'nuff will."

Maybe I didn't have nothing to show for it, but for the way it made me feel inside, that was the best darn ten cents I ever spent.

FIFTEEN

Mama was in a real snit when I got home.

"Will ya look at this?" she said, waving an envelope in front of my face. "Stubborn, prideful fool," she muttered as I took the envelope from her hand.

"It's from Pa!" I said, my heart leaping.

"Aye," said Mama, her arms crossed, her foot tapping the floor.

Then I discovered what it was that got her goat so. In the envelope, along with the note, were the three dollars Mama had hidden in his sack. I read the note:

> Dearest Molly,
>
> It'll be a cold day in hell before I'll eat a meal that's been stole from the mouths of my wife and children.
>
> Your devoted,
> Daniel

I couldn't help smiling.

"And just what are you grinnin' at?" asked Mama.

I shrugged. "Well, that's Pa for you," I said.

"Aaagh," said Mama, throwing her hands up in the air. "I mighta known you'd take his side."

Our door buzzer rang and Ma made a face. "Now who the devil is that?" she mumbled.

"I'll go see, Ma." I went into the front room, pushed the window up, and stuck my head out. "Who's down there?" I yelled. The front door opened and Mr. Twiddle stepped out onto the stoop and looked up. I frowned.

"Twiddle," he yelled, "collecting."

"Yeah, just a minute," I told him. I couldn't stand Mr. Twiddle. Not that he's a bad guy or anything, but he's an insurance man. Every week, for no reason that I can see, we have to give him a quarter, for which we get absolutely nothing. Some racket, if you ask me.

"It's Twiddle," I told Ma, and she made a face, too.

"Don't give it to him, Ma," I said. "Who cares if we have insurance."

"No, no," Ma said with a sigh. "Insurance is important." She reached up over the sink and took down the jar where we kept my shoeshine money. She took out five nickels and handed them to me. "Go pay him, please, Danny."

I dropped the nickels down one by one and watched Mr. Twiddle put them in his pocket—nickels it had taken me the better part of a week to earn. He smiled when he caught the last one and tipped his hat. "See you next week," he yelled.

"Yeah, sure." I could hardly wait.

I heard a door slam and looked over to see Mickey dashing down his front steps. He saw me hanging out the window.

"Hey, Garvey," he yelled. "Let's go. We're gonna be late again!"

Oh no. I glanced at the clock on the front room wall. Five minutes to ten! I raced through my room, grabbed my missal, and shot past Ma and out the door. "Gonna be late for catechism," I yelled over my shoulder.

Mickey and I ran to the corner, turned left, and kept going right on through the tunnel and down 106th. The sidewalk was full of Saturday morning shoppers. We zigged and zagged around them and arrived at St. Cecilia's, all out of breath, just a minute past ten.

Sister Mary Francis pursed her lips and stared at us with her beady black eyes when we walked in.

"We're late again, I see," she said.

An irresistible urge to sully came over me.

"Oh? Were you late, too, Sister?" I asked.

I'd been tempted to say it a million times, every time she referred to me as "we," but I'd always managed to keep my mouth shut. Now I'd gone and done it. A rash of giggles burst out in the room and Sister's eyes flew open wide.

"Master Garvey," she said, "*you* will spend the class on your knees in front of the room."

Another giggle swept the room.

"And the next one who makes a sound will join Master Garvey."

There was absolute silence as I took up my position on the cold, cement floor. I tried to lean back on my heels, but Sister gave me a sharp rap on the rump with her pointer.

"At attention!" she said.

One of the girls burst out laughing.

"Miss Riley," said Sister, "join Master Garvey, please."

Wow, Sister must've really been in a lousy mood. I'd never seen her make a *girl* kneel before. Maggie appeared beside me, trying to look repentant, but not quite succeeding.

"Anyone else?" Sister demanded.

Absolute silence reigned again.

"All right," said Sister, "open your missals, please."

As soon as Sister's back was turned, Maggie stuffed a note into my hand. I unfolded it quietly and read it.

Dear Danny,

I saw you naked in the tub last night.

—Maggie

"Master Garvey!"

"Uh . . . yes, Sister?"

"Would you care to read your note for the class please?"

"Uh . . . no, Sister. I really don't think—"

"Read it!"

"Yes, ma'am."

SIXTEEN

Maggie and I each got assigned five full rosaries to be said before bedtime. In addition, because I happen to be the boy, which automatically makes me the guilty one in Sister's eyes, I got to endure Sister's idea of the ultimate torture. I had to pull my pants legs up and kneel on the floor for the rest of the class with my bare knees in a pile of uncooked rice. It's a pretty good torture, believe me.

"I'm gonna kill her," I told Mickey as I hobbled up the stairs after class. "One of these days I'm gonna kill her."

"Sister?"

"No—Maggie."

Mickey laughed. "Oh yeah," he said. "Well, not today. Today you're gonna ask her to the movies, remember?"

I pushed the door open and stepped out into the bright sunshine. "Not on your life," I told Mickey.

He grabbed my collar and pulled my face up to his. "A deal is a deal, Garvey," he said. "You still owe me."

I pushed him away and bent down to rub my aching knees. "Yeah, yeah," I said. "But I won't forget this, Mickey. Just wait 'til next time *you* owe *me*."

"Sure, sure. Look, here they come. You do the asking."

"Me!"

"Just do it, Garvey."

Maggie and Kitty came out of the church giggling hysterically. Mickey shoved me right out in front of them.

"Oh, Danny," said Maggie, going off into another fit of laughter, "you were so-o-o funny. I thought Sister was going to faint on the spot."

"Oh yeah, real funny," I said. "It's gonna be real funny spending Saturday night saying rosaries, too, isn't it?"

Maggie burst out laughing again. "Oh come on," she said. "You're not really gonna do it, are you?"

I stared at her. It had never occurred to me *not* to.

"Aren't *you*?" I asked.

"Of course not, silly."

"But it'll be a mortal sin."

"Oh, Danny." She laughed again. "You are so-o-o funny."

The way she kept laughing made me mad, like she thought I was some kind of a little kid or something. I stuck out my chest. "Of course I'm not gonna say it," I said, all the time trembling inside, waiting to be struck dead on the spot.

"Oh yeah, I'll bet," said Maggie.

Mickey stepped forward and bumped me in the shoulder. I didn't say anything. He bumped me harder.

"Well, see you later," said Maggie. She and Kitty started to walk away.

Mickey bumped me so hard I practically fell over.

I scowled at him, then yelled after the girls, "Hey. Wait a minute."

Maggie stopped and looked back. Mickey and Kitty glanced at each other, turned red, and then both stared down at the sidewalk.

"Yea, what?" asked Maggie.

"You . . . uh . . . wanna go to the mfff-ffff," I mumbled.

"To the what?"

"The *movies*," I said, my face burning. "Do you want to go to the movies with Mickey and me?"

Maggie looked at me like I was crazy.

"Why?" she asked.

"Beats me," I said.

Mickey gave me another shove.

Maggie looked at him, then she looked at Kitty, who was still staring at the sidewalk, her face beet-red.

Maggie started to grin. "Oh, I get it," she said. "Well . . . I don't know. What's playing?"

"You know what's playing. Tom Mix in—"

Mickey suddenly grabbed my arm and yanked me off balance. That did it. Owe him or not, I'd had it.

"Look," I said. "You touch me one more time and I'm gonna break every bone in your body."

"All right, all right. Shush, will you?"

He steered me to one side and whispered in my ear, "We're not taking them to the matinee, dummy. We're taking them to the *real* show."

"Why?"

"Because I said so."

"But what about the serial? I gotta see what happens."

"Ask somebody."

"Come on, Mick."

"Look, Danny, we're going to see *A Farewell to Arms,* and that's that."

"*A Farewell to Arms!* That's nothing but a sob story."

"I know." Mickey grinned and made his voice even lower. "Girls love that stuff. Tony Maretti took his girl to see it, and she let him put his arm around her all the way home."

"Well, whoopie," I said.

"Grow up, Garvey, and just go tell 'em."

"Why don't *you* tell 'em, if you're so smooth?"

"Because you owe—"

"Yeah, yeah, I know."

I turned back to the girls. "We're gonna see *A Farewell to Arms,*" I said.

Maggie's eyes lit up. "You mean that movie with Helen Hayes and Gary Cooper?"

I looked at Mickey. He nodded.

"Yup," I said.

Maggie looked at Kitty. Kitty gave her a shy, sideways smile. Maggie looked at me again.

"You payin'?"

"Yup."

"Popcorn and sodas, too?"

Mickey nodded.

"Yup."

"Wow . . . sure," said Maggie. "What time?"

"Oh, about six-thirty," said Mickey, suddenly finding his voice.

"Great," said Maggie. "See you then."

She and Kitty put their heads together and giggled, then ran off toward home. We watched them go, then Mickey gave me another nudge.

"Hey, Dan?"

"What?"

"Did she really see you naked?"

SEVENTEEN

A knock came on our door at exactly six-thirty. "I'll get it, Ma," I yelled. "It's probably Mick." I pulled the door open, and there stood the funniest sight I'd ever seen. Mickey had on a slouch hat, somebody's ratty old raccoon coat that was so big it was dragging on the ground, a shirt and tie, knickers, and argyle socks. "You must be pulling my leg," I said, trying not to laugh.

"What?" asked Mickey. "What's the problem?" He strode past me into the room, and I practically choked on the smell of dime-store cologne.

"Well, Michael," said Mama, "don't you look like the cat's meow."

"The cat's meow?" I snorted. "He looks like a vaudeville clown."

"Now, Danny, don't be rude," said Mama. "I think Michael looks just lovely."

"Yeah, that's how he looks, okay, just lovely. You are *just lovely,* Michael."

Mickey squeezed his hand into a fist.

"That'll be enough, Daniel," said Mama. "It wouldn't hurt you to dress up a bit."

"Yeah," said Mickey. "Get changed, will you. You were supposed to be ready by now."

"What's wrong with what I got on?" I asked.

"You been playin' stickball all afternoon and ya smell," said Mama. "Go change yer shirt at least."

It was two against one, and I could see I wasn't gonna win, so I filled up the washbowl and carried it back to my room. By the time I came out again, Mickey was pacing back and forth.

"Will you hurry up," he said. "We're late."

"Hold your horses," I said. "You're the one who wanted me to change."

I kissed Ma good-bye and she looked at me funny.

"Your first date," she said, making a face like she was either gonna laugh or cry but couldn't decide which.

"It ain't a date," I said, grabbing my hat off the icebox and my jacket off its hook.

"You come home right after the show, now," Mama called after us. "Yer too young to be roamin' the streets at night."

Kitty answered the door, blushing beet-red again. She had on her Sunday dress, a ribbon in her hair, and real silk stockings! They must've been her mother's, the way they bagged around the ankles, but they only had a couple of runs in them and I couldn't believe Mrs. Riley was letting her wear them.

The three of us stood there tongue-tied, trying to think of something to say while the rest of the little Rileys stood around giggling at us. Finally Maggie and her mother came out of the bedroom. Good old Maggie had on her everyday jumper and knee socks. At least somebody was still normal.

We said our good-byes and Mickey and Kitty started down the stairs, Mickey's coat dragging behind him like a royal robe. I jerked my thumb at him behind his back and rolled my eyes at Maggie. She burst out laughing.

Mickey looked back. "What's so funny?" he asked.

"Nothing," she said.

Mickey turned his back again. This time Maggie pointed at him and held her nose, and *I* burst out laughing. Mickey stopped in his tracks. He came back up the stairs and grabbed my arm.

"Will you ladies excuse us?" he said.

Maggie and Kitty giggled as he steered me toward the back of the hall.

"Listen, *Junior*," he whispered. "I know this is asking a lot, but could you try not to act like a child, just for tonight?"

"Well, pardon me, *Mister* Crowley," I said. "I guess I forgot you're a *man* now."

"That's right. You wanna make something of it?"

I laughed. "I'm twice the man you are, Crowley."

"Then act it," said Mickey. He walked over and

took Kitty's arm, and they started down the stairs again.

Junior. Huh! What was eating him? I shoved my hands into my pockets and walked past Maggie. "Let's go," I said.

The movie was just as lousy as I expected, some drippy love story about an ambulance driver and a nurse during the war. I couldn't believe we'd passed up Tom Mix and a Hoot Gibson serial for this. The nurse dies in the end and I thought the whole theater was gonna get flooded with all the drippin' and snifflin' going on. I looked over and saw that Mickey had his arm around Kitty. He nodded toward Maggie like I ought to do the same, and I gave him a look like I'd rather eat worms. I poked Maggie and nodded in their direction, expecting her to laugh, but she just gave me an annoyed look and dabbed at her eyes with the sleeve of her blouse.

Mickey and Kitty held hands on the way home, and Maggie acted real funny. She was quiet for a long time and sighed a lot, then she started saying things like, "Wasn't that just the most romantic movie you've ever seen?" and "Aren't the stars beautiful tonight?" I'd never seen Maggie act like that before. I didn't know what to say to her.

We passed one of those Dime-a-Dance parlors.

"Oh look," said Maggie, grabbing my sleeve and pulling me over to the window. There was a row of ladies sitting on chairs, and every time the music started a bunch of fellas came over and picked out a girl and paid a dime to dance with her. It was a real waste of money if you asked me.

"Isn't it wonderful?" said Maggie. "As soon as I'm old enough, I'm gonna get a job at one of these places." The band started playing "Someone to Watch Over Me," and she wrapped her arms around herself and started swaying dreamily around the sidewalk. I pictured her dancing with one of those fellas, and I didn't like it.

"What would you wanna do a dumb thing like that for?" I asked her.

"It's just *so* romantic," said Maggie, "all those swell gentlemen paying for the privilege of having a dance."

The way she said "gentlemen" made me mad, like she thought I was some kind of flat tire or something.

"Oh yeah," I said, "well what makes you think any *gentleman* would pay to dance with you?"

Maggie turned and smiled at me. She didn't say anything. She didn't have to. With her dark hair shining on her shoulders and her blue eyes reflecting the light from the streetlamps, she was beautiful. When did she get so beautiful? When did she get so tall? It seems like lately everyone is getting tall, except me.

"Well, you wouldn't catch me payin' to dance with no bean pole," I told her.

Maggie just kept looking at me and smiling. She put her face very close to mine. "Don't you worry, Danny Garvey," she whispered. "You'll grow."

The way she said it, so soft and breathless, her

eyes staring straight into mine, made my mouth go dry and my ears start to burn.

Then suddenly she giggled and ran off up the street after Mickey and Kitty.

"Oh yeah?" I shouted after her. "Well, who asked ya?"

EIGHTEEN

Mama was listening to the radio and writing to Pa again when I came in.

"Aren't those letters piling up some?" I asked.

Mama just shrugged and smiled.

"I'm just tellin' yer daddy about yer date. How was it?"

"It wasn't a date," I said. "And it stunk."

There was a sudden loud crash from across the hall, and then the sound of yelling.

Mama winced. "He's been at it all evenin'," she said. "I was hopin' he'd stop once the girls got home."

There was another loud crash, followed by a muffled scream. Mama jumped up and we rushed into the hall. Mrs. Mahoney was thumping down the stairs, her forehead creased with worry. We could hear the little Riley kids whimpering.

"No, Pa . . . Please!" I heard Maggie cry.

"Shuddup or you'll be next," came her father's slurred reply.

I banged on the door and rattled the knob. It was locked.

"Mind yer own business," Mr. Riley shouted. There was another crash and some more screaming and sobbing.

"Danny," Mama whispered, "run for a policeman."

I hesitated, not wanting to leave them all.

"Run, Danny," she insisted, "before it's too late."

I dashed down the stairs, past the other tenants, who were starting to gather in the halls, and out into the street. There were no cops in sight. The police station was over on 104th between Lexington and Park. I started running in that direction, when out of the corner of my eye I spied a blue uniform coming out of the tunnel on 105th.

"Officer," I shouted. "Officer—hurry!"

The policeman's head went up at the sound of my voice and he ran to meet me, his heavy black shoes echoing dully off the pavement. I was glad to see that it was Pete Murray. Pete grew up in our neighborhood and knows us all, which saved me a lot of explaining.

"Danny," he said when he got close enough to recognize me, "what's wrong?"

"It's Mr. Riley again."

Pete nodded and rushed past me. I hurried after him. When we reached the building the tenants parted to let us through. Mama still stood by the Rileys' door,

Mrs. Mahoney by her side. They both had tears in their eyes.

"Oh, Peter, thank the Lord," said Mama when she saw Officer Murray. "He's surely gone crazy this time."

Officer Murray banged on the door.

"Open up, Riley," he shouted. "It's the law."

"Go ta hell," came the answer.

"Officer, please help—"

The voice, Maggie's, was silenced by a loud slap.

"Break the door down," I shouted. "I'll help you."

"That won't be necessary," said Officer Murray. He took a skeleton key from a ring on his belt and opened the lock. The door opened a crack and stopped again, held by a chain. Officer Murray frowned. "Let's try the front-room door," he said.

Mama shook her head. "They've got an extra bolt on it," she said. "The girls sleep in there."

Officer Murray tried it anyway, but it wouldn't budge.

"All right, Danny," he said to me, "you can give me that hand now."

He jammed his billy club into the crack in the kitchen door and used it as a wedge, throwing his weight against it. I threw my shoulder against the door just below his.

"Okay, now!" he shouted.

We shoved with all our strength. We heard a crack, but the door held.

"Again," shouted Officer Murray.

We shoved again, and this time Mama and Mrs.

Mahoney threw their weight against our backs. I pushed so hard I thought my veins were going to pop, then all of a sudden there was a splintering sound and the door burst open, tumbling the lot of us into the room.

Mr. Riley staggered over to the stove, grabbed one of Mrs. Riley's irons, and lunged at Pete Murray. Luckily, though, Mr. Riley was so drunk and clumsy that Pete easily rolled out of the way and jumped to his feet. One blow of the billy club sent the iron crashing to the floor, and the next thing we knew, Officer Murray had Mr. Riley bent over the kitchen table and was snapping his wrists into handcuffs.

Mama got up and went over to help Kitty with Mrs. Riley, who was slumped on the floor beside the icebox, her hands covering her face. Maggie, an angry red welt below her right eye, comforted the little Rileys who huddled together in the corner, sobbing quietly.

"Mrs. Riley," said Officer Murray, when he had Mr. Riley fully secured, "what do you want me to do?"

Mrs. Riley spoke from behind her hands, her voice trembling and tearful. "Fix it," she said, "so he can never set foot in this apartment again."

Mr. Riley never flinched. He stared straight ahead, his eyes red and watery, his mouth set in a hard line. I saw Maggie look at him. Tears filled her eyes, then she caught my gaze and quickly looked away again.

Officer Murray steered Mr. Riley to the door. "I'll

send someone up to fix this," he said, "and I'll come by with the papers in the morning."

Mrs. Riley nodded, still behind her hands.

"Danny," said Mama, after Officer Murray and Mr. Riley were gone, "help Mrs. Mahoney upstairs and tell the neighbors they can go back to bed now. Everything is all right."

I did as Mama asked. When I came back down Mrs. Riley was sitting at the table. Her eyes were swollen black and blue, and blood oozed from a cut on her cheek. She dabbed at the tears that streamed from her eyes with a crumpled handkerchief.

"Oh, Molly," she said sadly, "what's become of our men?"

Mama looked up at me.

"Go on home to bed now, Danny," she said gently. "I'll be along shortly."

"Aw, Ma."

"Go on with ya now, and check on Maureen."

"Yes ma'am."

NINETEEN

～

Maureen was sleeping soundly, totally unaware of anything that had happened. I lay down on my bed, but my stomach hurt and my mind kept trying to make some sense of everything I had just seen.

Folks around here have been making allowances for Mr. Riley as long as I can remember. He grew up just a couple of blocks from here, his parents Irish immigrants like Ma and Pa. People say he had a fine wit and a good heart and everyone was fond of him. He fell in love with Maggie's mom, except she wasn't Maggie's mom yet, of course. Her name was Katherine Gerky then, and she lived in the neighborhood, too. They were all set to get married when our country got itself mixed up in the World War, and Mr. Riley and most of the other guys in the neighborhood ended up in the army.

Mr. Riley came home from the war, but a lot of

his friends didn't. Folks say Mr. Riley was never the same again. "Shell-shocked," they call it. He's never worked much. The Rileys have been on relief long as I can remember. Mr. Riley just lies around the apartment or hangs out down on the stoop, drinking Mrs. Riley's homemade beer and sponging off her and the kids. Sometimes, like tonight, he gets ahold of a bottle of bootleg whiskey, and then there's real trouble.

I felt like hating him after what he'd done to Maggie and her ma tonight, but that didn't seem fair. After all, it wasn't his fault he went off and got shell-shocked. But whose fault was it then?

After what seemed like a long time I heard the kitchen door open and close, and the rattle of the chain latch sliding over. I'd left the bedroom door curtain open, and I saw Mama come into her room and bend over the crib at the foot of her bed. She stood for a long time that way, smoothing Maureen's blanket and stroking her hair. Then she sat down in her rocker and put her head in her hands. I heard her sigh deeply.

"Mama? Are you okay?"

She looked up.

"Danny?" she whispered. "I thought you'd be asleep by now."

"I can't sleep."

Mama came in and sat on the edge of my bed. She smoothed back my hair and caressed my cheek.

"I know," she said. "Such an awful thing for a child to see."

"I'm not a child anymore, Ma."

She looked at me sadly. "No," she said. "I don't s'pose you are, but 'twas an awful thing to see, just the same."

"Why did Mrs. Riley marry him," I asked, "if he was shell-shocked like people say?"

"Because she loved him, Danny, and she thought her love could bring him around again. Seemed like it might, too, for a time. He straightened out some after Maggie and Kitty were born, worked hard, stayed clear o' the bottle. . . ."

Mama smiled a faraway smile. "Those were good times," she said. "We did everything together, the Rileys and us. Do you remember at all? You were just a wee bit of a thing."

"I remember the picnics at Coney Island and the trips to the zoo."

"Do ya then? Good. Try to remember Johnny Riley that way, Danny, not the way you saw him tonight."

"But what went wrong, Ma?" I asked. "Why did he change back again?"

"I guess something wasn't healed inside him," Mama said. "When the other babies started coming, one after the other, times got hard for the Rileys. Mr. Riley started fallin' apart, little by little. Then the depression came. . . ."

Mama stopped talking. She stared out the window into the darkness of the alley.

"Something wrong?" I asked.

She shook her head, but her eyes were glazed and far away. "Hard times," she said softly. "I thought it would be different here." Then she looked at me and laughed a little at herself. "That's the Irish in me, I guess, always lookin' for that pot o' gold."

I smiled. "Are you ever sorry you left Ireland, Ma?" I asked.

"Oh, I miss it sure enough. It was such a lovely green place, and family all around. But no, I wouldn't go back. I was wrong to say it isn't different here. It is. Yer pa has learned to read and taken up a trade. You're gettin' an education and Maureen will, too, even though she's but a girl. Everyone has a chance here, no matter how poor. Why, you could even grow up to be president, like that Mr. Lincoln, if you wanted to bad enough."

I had to laugh. "An Irish Catholic president! You are a dreamer, Ma."

Mama stiffened at my words.

"Aye," she said with a toss of her head. "It's dreamers make the world go round, and don't ya forget it."

"Sorry," I said. "I was just teasing."

Mama relaxed again and took my hand in both of hers. "I know," she said, squeezing it tight. Then suddenly she held my hand up, as if to see it better. "What's this?" she said. "You been growin' again?"

I snorted. "I doubt it, Ma."

"Yes, yes ya have. Look here now. Yer hand is bigger than mine."

"Really?" I spread my fingers out to measure against hers. "Wow," I said. "Keen."

Mama laughed. "Never ya mind," she said. "Don't

be springin' such surprises on yer poor mother. Next you'll be tellin' me yer too big to hear a story."

I smiled at her. "Never, Ma."

Even Pa loves Ma's stories. Ma's grandfather was a *seanachie,* a storyteller, back in Ireland, and Mama has "the gift."

"Get under the covers then," she said, "and close yer eyes."

I did as she told me, happy to let her take me back with her to the hills of Ireland, hills I know as well in my mind as the streets of New York. They're magic hills, full of fairies and leprechauns and pots of gold, but they're scary, too, haunted by ghosts and the scream of the banshee. Most of all though, they're Mama's hills and Pa's too, which somehow makes them mine as well. I never tire of hearing about them.

"And I told yer Uncle Tomas," Mama was saying, " 'Don't take yer eyes from him, not for a minute, and I'll run get the spade.' I ran like the banshee was chasin' me, but when I got back the leprechaun was gone just the same, and there was yer Uncle Tomas, sleepin' like a babe."

I laughed. "So the leprechaun tricked you out of the gold again?"

"Aye, that he did."

Mama sat back a little and her eyes grew dreamy. "That night," she said, "as we were lyin' on our pallets in the byre, your Uncle Tomas turned to me. 'Molly,' he said, 'if we'da got that pot o' gold, and ya could have anything in the world, what would ya choose?' "

Mama looked at me and her eyes sparkled. "Can ya guess what I said?"

"No, Mama, what?"

"A pitcher of cream." She tossed her head and laughed at herself. "How's that," she said, "for a child's wildest dream? A pitcher of cream . . ."

TWENTY

Sunday, October 23, 1932

"Danny? What're ya doin' on the floor, lad? Did ya fall out of bed?"

Mama's voice startled me awake, and I sat up, trying to figure out where I was.

"Danny?" she said again. "Did ya fall out of bed?"

"Uh . . . no, Mama. I was saying my prayers. . . . I guess I fell asleep on my knees."

"Poor dear," she said. "Such a good boy. You'll have to hurry now, though, or we'll be late for Mass."

"Okay, Ma."

I didn't tell her that the prayers I was saying were my penance for sassing Sister at catechism yesterday. As a matter of fact, I'd forgotten all about them in the excitement of last night. Then I had this dream that Sister was chasing me through the sewers, throwing flowers at me. I woke up in a cold sweat, sure it must be some kind of bad omen or something.

So I got down on my knees and started in, only I was so tired that I kept falling face forward into the sheets. The next thing I knew, Ma was waking me up. I still didn't know if I was done or not, so I said the rosary to myself the whole time I was getting dressed and all during breakfast and all the way to church, just to be safe.

We saw the Rileys at Mass. Maggie and her mother both had on those kind of hats with the little veils that come down over your face. Ma invited them all over for Sunday dinner and Mrs. Riley nodded. After Mass, Ma gave me a quarter and sent me to the bakery to buy buns for supper.

"Spend the whole quarter," she said.

I stared at her. "The whole quarter, on buns?"

"Aye," she said. "The Rileys will be stayin' the afternoon, I'm sure."

"But . . . the whole quarter?"

"Aye," Mama repeated. "I'm thinkin' we all deserve a bit of a treat. Go along with you now."

"Okay, Ma."

The bakery was crowded, but I didn't mind the wait. Standing there, surrounded by all those good things to eat, breathing in that sweet, buttery air was about as close as you could get to heaven without dying. When my turn came I looked over the buns. There were cheese, raspberry, apple, lemon, cinnamon . . . ten kinds in all. "I'll have two of each," I said, feeling very rich as I pushed the quarter across the counter.

It started to rain on the way home and I tucked

the buns under my jacket to keep them dry. Their warmth felt good against my chest. Mama was bustling around the kitchen when I came in. A huge pot of chicken soup boiled on the stove.

"Run up and tell poor old Mrs. Mahoney to join us," Mama said. She always calls Mrs. Mahoney "poor old Mrs. Mahoney." I'm not really sure why. She doesn't seem that poor or that old. I think it's got something to do with her wooden leg or her being a widow or maybe both.

"No sense in her spending the day alone up there," Mama went on, "when one more or less down here won't make a bit o' difference."

Mrs. Mahoney was delighted. She asked me to carry her box of beadwork down for her, and she followed with a pot of "tea" tucked under her arm. Mrs. Mahoney supports herself by doing piecework, making beaded pocketbooks at home. I don't know how much she makes, but she pays us kids two cents a pocketbook to help out, and we're always glad to get it. Whenever we have some free time we go up and sit in her kitchen and string beads, and she tells us tales of when she was young and her husband was alive. Her husband was a merchant marine, and when they were first married Mrs. Mahoney used to sail all around the world with him. She says that's how she lost her leg. It was bitten off by a shark one time when she was washed overboard in a gale. Mama winks and says Mrs. Mahoney is just giving us a bit of the blarney.

When we came down, the Rileys were marching

across the hall like a little line of ducks, all carrying chairs and dishes and glasses and such. Maggie and Kitty brought up the rear, struggling with their extra table. I put the beadwork down and gave them a hand. We pushed their table and ours together and soon the meal was set—steaming bowls of chicken soup, thick with vegetables; loaves of good, chewy bread; butter; and fresh milk—a real feast.

I've always loved Sunday afternoons. Sunday is the one day of the week that we have all we can eat. Even if there's nothing but oatmeal for the rest of the week, Ma always manages to put together a big meal for Sunday dinner, followed later in the evening by a supper of sweet buns and hot chocolate. It's a day for resting and visiting, too. One or more of the neighbor families always drop by, and the women sit in the front room knitting or doing piecework, talking and sipping "tea," while the men sit in the kitchen playing cards and drinking homemade beer. The smaller kids roll and tumble in the bedrooms, and us older ones drift from front to back, keeping peace, sneaking sips, and listening in on all the gossip and laughter. It's really keen, and even though we're poor, I can't imagine that rich people are any happier than we are on Sunday afternoons.

Today there were no men playing cards, so we all stayed in the kitchen where it was warm.

"No sense lighting the kerosene heater in the front room," Mama said.

It felt strangely quiet at first, in spite of the crowd, and we all seemed to be talking extra loud and laughing extra hard to fill up the room. By the end of dinner, though, everyone had relaxed and things seemed almost normal. The dishes were cleared away, Maureen and Marion put down for their naps, and the smaller kids sent across the hall to play where their noise wouldn't wake the babies.

Ma made hot chocolate for Maggie, Kitty, and me and poured more tea for herself and the ladies. Then we all set to work on the pocketbooks. I was glad Mickey wasn't around. He won't make pocketbooks anymore. He says it's sissy work. If you ask me, two cents is two cents. And anyway, what else are you gonna do on a rainy Sunday afternoon? Besides, it's a good excuse to sit there and listen to the grown-ups talk. They can say some pretty funny things when they get to laughing and passing that teapot around.

Today the talk was full of politics, with the election just a couple of weeks away.

"They say it's going to be a rout," said Mrs. Mahoney.

"Aye, and well it should," said Mama, her cheeks flushing with anger. "That man has no right in the White House. It's out on the streets he belongs, in one of his own Hoovervilles, and then see how he feels about the depression!"

Hoovervilles are what they call the little shanty-towns that have sprung up all over the country since the depression began; makeshift towns thrown together by homeless, out-of-work folks. I haven't seen any, 'cause Ma won't let me go near, but there's supposed to be one in Central Park and another over between Riverside Drive and the river. Folks are living in shacks made out of just about anything they can find, I guess.

"Him that was supposed to be such a great humanitarian," said Mrs. Mahoney with a huff, "feeding all the hungry in Europe after the war. How can he turn his back on his own people now?"

"Daniel says Hoover's for government staying out of business," Mama said, "for lettin' the economy straighten out by itself. But I say, how long can we wait?"

"How long, indeed?" said Mrs. Mahoney. "Does he want to see every man, woman, and child out on the streets?"

Mrs. Riley, who had been very quiet, shook her head. "It's time for new ideas," she said. "Roosevelt is for the ordinary man, for helping the farmers and putting folks back to work. We need a down-to-earth man like him in the White House."

"Aye," Mama agreed. "Hoover's got his head in the clouds."

There was a sudden ruckus across the hall, and a pile of little Rileys came bursting into the room, shouting and swatting each other and waking up Marion and Maureen.

"All right, all right," said Mrs. Riley when the three women had gotten things calmed down some. "Now tell me what's the matter."

"Johnny won't be the daddy," yelled seven-year-old Alice. "He wants to be the mommy."

Johnny stood with a doll under his arm and his bottom lip stuck out.

"I always have to be the daddy," he said. "I don't want to be the daddy anymore. The daddy always gets drunk and goes to jail."

Mrs. Riley put her hand to her mouth. Her eyes filled with tears, and she looked away. Mama and Mrs. Mahoney glanced awkwardly at one another.

I looked at Johnny, standing there clutching the doll. Poor kid. Bad enough he had all them sisters to put up with. Now he didn't even have a pa to set him straight.

"C'mon, Johnny," I said, putting my pocketbook aside. "I want to show you something." I took his hand and led him into my room.

"Look, goofy," I said, hoisting him up onto my bed. "You're not cut out to be a mommy, take it from me." I pulled the doll out from under his arm. "Haven't you got any boy toys?"

"Sure," he said, bristling up. "I got a fire engine."

"Well, that's good," I said. "That's real good. But you know what? I got something better than that. I got a Jack Armstrong whistle ring."

His eyes opened wide. "No foolin'?"

I went over to my bureau and pulled my cigar box full of treasures out of the top drawer. I slipped the ring onto my finger and blew. A shrill whistle sounded. I had sent away for it a few years ago for a couple of Wheaties boxtops. Jack Armstrong was my hero back then. I put the ring into Johnny's hand.

"You want it?" I asked.

"No foolin'?" he repeated.

"No foolin'."

"Wowwee! Sure." He sprang from the bed and was about to charge out of the room.

"Hold on . . . hold on there just a minute," I said, grabbing his sleeve and pulling him back. "There's a few conditions, you know."

He turned his big blue eyes slowly up to mine, fearful, I guess, that I wasn't really gonna give it to him.

I smiled. "If you're gonna wear a ring like that," I said, "you gotta live up to it. You gotta promise to be an all-American boy, like Jack—brave and honest and strong."

"I promise," he said, eyes shining.

"And no more sissy talk."

"You bet."

"Okay," I said, handing him back the doll. "Now go give this to your sister."

"You bet," he shouted again. "Hey Ma, look what Danny gave me!"

I looked up to see Maggie standing in the doorway as he charged by. She smiled.

"Thanks," she said. It was the first word either of us had spoken to each other since last night.

I shrugged. "Just didn't want him growing up to be no sissy, that's all," I said. I didn't tell her what I'd really been thinking. Maybe little Johnny wasn't half wrong. Why should he want to be a man when all the men he saw were useless? The way things were going, men would probably be extinct, like dinosaurs, by the time we grew up.

Maggie came over and bent to look into my treasure box. She picked out a small rubber stamp.

"A Tom Mix branding iron," she said, laughing and holding it up. "I wanted one of these so bad, but Ma wouldn't let us buy the Ralston unless we promised to eat it all." She made a face.

"Yeah," I told her. "Ma made me eat it, too—two whole boxes!" I stuck my tongue out and shivered at the memory.

We both laughed.

Maggie bent and put the stamp back into the box, then straightened up slowly and looked around the room. "Remember how we used to play Wild Bill Hickok in here with our rubber-band guns?"

"Sure I do, you low-down sidewinder you."

Maggie laughed again, then her smile faded. She ran her hand along the iron bed rail. "Seems like a long time ago," she said.

I looked at her and knew what she was thinking.

"I'm sorry," I said, "about your pa."

She turned toward me, but her eyes seemed to look beyond me, at something sad and faraway. "Yeah," she said softly.

TWENTY-ONE

～⚮～

Tuesday, November 8, 1932

Over two weeks have gone by with no further word
from Pa.

"He could send a postcard at least," I told Mama
at breakfast. "It'd only cost a penny."

"A penny's a penny," said Mama. "If you haven't
got one, ya can no more buy a postcard than a T-
bone steak."

I looked down at my oatmeal. I didn't like to think
of Pa wandering around without a penny in his pocket.

"C'mon now," said Mama gently. "Eat yer breakfast. Sure an' we'll be hearin' any day now."

"Aren't you gonna eat?" I asked. Mama was feeding Maureen from a bowl of oatmeal, but there was
nothing in front of her place but a cup of tea.

"I haven't much of an appetite this mornin'."

"Nor yesterday? Nor the day before?" I looked at
her closely. She seemed paler than usual, and there

131

were dark circles under her eyes. "Are you feelin' all right, Ma?"

She laughed nervously. "Of course I am."

A vague fear crept into my belly, but it was too scary to think about. Not now. Not with Pa gone. "Are you sure?"

"Sure an' I'm sure. Just got me a little touch of the flu is all. Mrs. Mahoney had it last week, if you recall."

I breathed a little sigh of relief. "Oh yeah. Well, why don't you go back to bed then? With school closed today I can watch Maureen."

Mama huffed. "I've no intention of spending election day in bed. I'm doin' just fine, thank you, but as soon as you finish your breakfast you *can* watch Maureen while I go cast my vote."

"Votin' for Hoover, are you?" I asked, just to get her goat.

"Aye," she said, "when pigs fly."

I laughed. Ma doesn't usually care much for politics, but she's really riled up about this election. She's been favoring Roosevelt right along, but I think it was that Bonus March business this past summer that really turned her against Hoover.

"To think," she always says, "our own president setting the army against the poor veterans that fought for this country in the war. Unarmed men killed, and that dear innocent little baby!"

It seems a bunch of veterans of the World War had got together and walked with their families to Washington, D.C., to ask if the president would let them have the bonuses the army owed them a little early—to help them get through the depression. Instead of meeting with them, Hoover sent General MacArthur with his troops and tanks and everything to turn them away. Trouble broke out and several marchers were shot and killed. The troops carried bayonets and threw tear gas grenades. A little boy was stabbed through the leg, and a baby, who'd been born on the march, died from the gas.

Mama's been saying rosaries for that baby ever since. Bernard Myers was his name. I asked her once if rosaries would work on a Jewish baby.

"Daniel," she said, "are you forgettin' that our Lord was a Jewish baby?"

When Mama got back from the polls her cheeks were pink again. "Everyone is votin' for Roosevelt," she said, hugging me happily. "Oh, Danny, I know he's gonna win."

"And then things will get better, and Pa will come home."

"Aye." Her eyes sparkled. "Pa will come home."

A knock came on the door. "Ready?" yelled Mickey's voice.

I grabbed my broomstick. "Yeah," I called back. Then I turned to Ma. "That is, if you don't need me anymore."

"No, run along," said Mama. "You won't have too many more chances to play stickball before the cold and the snow set in."

"You sure you're feelin' okay then?"

"Fit as a fiddle. Off with you now."

I grabbed up my ball and joined Mickey in the hall. When we got downstairs he pulled me aside.

"Can you keep a secret?" he whispered.

"Sure. What?"

"C'mon. I gotta show you something."

He led me across the gutter to the wall on the other side. There were benches all along where bums usually slept at night and mothers sat during the day, watching their little kids play. It was a little late in the morning for bums, and a little early for mothers, so most of the benches were empty. Mickey pulled me over to one of them and, after again swearing me to secrecy, pointed to something on the wall behind it. I looked closely. It was a heart chipped into the stone, and it had the initials "M. C. & K. R." in it.

"Holy cow," I said. "Who do you think did that?"

"I did," said Mickey.

"You did? Why on earth would you do that? What if somebody sees it? What if *she* sees it?"

"I want her to see it. I asked her if I could do it."

"You *asked* her? What'd she say?"

"She said yes, dummy."

"She said 'yes, dummy'?"

"No. She said yes. *You're* the dummy."

I shook my head. "I don't get it, Mickey. Six months ago you would've flattened anybody that wrote your initials in a heart with a girl's. Now you go and do it yourself—in stone yet! What's gotten into you?"

Mickey grinned and shrugged. "Love, I guess," he said.

"Aw c'mon," I told him. "I'm gonna throw up."

Mickey gave me a deadpan look. "Grow up, will you, Dan," he said.

I stared at him. "Are you serious?"

"Yup."

What else was there to say? I just stood there staring at him with my mouth hanging open until he burst out laughing.

"C'mon," he said, "the guys are waiting, and if you don't shut that mouth you're gonna start attracting flies."

We walked down the middle of the gutter toward 106th, swinging our broomstick bats and bouncing our balls. I looked over at Mickey. He just kept smiling that goofy smile.

"Love, huh?" I said.

"Yup."

Silence again.

"How do you know?"

"I just know."

"*How* do you know?"

Mickey stopped walking and gave me a smug grin. "Don't worry," he said. "When it happens, you'll know."

"Well I ain't losin' any sleep over it."

Mickey shook his head and walked away. He was acting so screwy. I couldn't tell if he was feeding me a line or what.

"Mick?"

"Yeah?"

"What's it like?"

Mickey put his head back and stared up at the sky. "It's *copacetic,* Dan," he said dreamily. "It's the swellest thing that ever happened to me. I just can't stop thinking about her, and when she lets me hold her hand, it's like . . . well . . . it's like Christmas and the Fourth of July and my birthday, all rolled up together."

"Jeez . . ."

"And Dan?"

"Yeah?"

"You breathe one word of this to the guys and I'll break every bone in your body."

OWOOOGA! OWOOGA!

Mickey and I each jumped about three feet. We don't get too many cars up in our part of the city, and the loud blast of the horn right behind us scared us half to death. We both scrambled for the sidewalk, and stood breathing heavy as a gleaming yellow Pierce Arrow went by.

"Wow," said Mickey. "Would you look at that?"

"I'm looking, I'm looking," I told him, my eyes nearly bugging out of my head. It was the most gorgeous car I had ever seen, long and sleek and dripping with chrome. The guy behind the wheel was some fancy dude with a white hat and suit and spiffy black shirt.

"Bootlegger," said Mickey.

"Gotta be," I agreed. "Who else has that kind of money?"

Mickey shook his head and whistled. "Maybe we oughta get into bootlegging, Dan," he said.

I laughed. "Oh sure," I told him. "That'd be just our luck—go into bootlegging just when Roosevelt gets elected, ends Prohibition, and puts all the bootleggers out of business."

Mickey laughed, too. He slid an arm around my shoulder. "You're right, Bugsy," he said in a fake gangster twang. "I guess we better find ourselves another racket."

TWENTY-TWO

❧

Wednesday, November 9, 1932

The radio woke me up this morning. Mama had turned it way up. "Happy days are here again!" it blared.

"Roosevelt won!" Mama shouted as I staggered out to the kitchen, rubbing the sleep from my eyes. "It was a landslide!"

When I went down on the street with my shoe-shine kit, everyone was in high spirits. In less than an hour, I made almost fifty cents. Folks seem to suddenly have a good feeling about themselves again.

In school we talked about Mr. Roosevelt's "New Deal" and what it could mean for the country. For the first time, the U.S. government is going to fund relief programs, instead of leaving it up to the states and cities. New public works and conservation programs will be started to put people back to work.

There will be national unemployment insurance, and farmers will be subsidized so that they can reduce their production and prices will stabilize.

I don't really understand what it all means, but Mr. Brewster, our social studies teacher, said it means help for the hungry and homeless, and most of all, jobs for the jobless. He warned us that it will all take time, of course—as if we didn't know. I figure that since Mr. Roosevelt isn't even gonna be inaugurated until March fourth, it will take at least until the summer before he gets the depression straightened out. That's okay though. As long as we know the end is in sight, I'm sure we can make it through the winter.

Mr. Weissman was in such a good mood when I got to the store that he gave me the afternoon off. I couldn't believe my good fortune as I headed for Mickey's building. The afternoon off! This really was turning out to be a great day. I met Mr. Moriarty, the undertaker, coming down Mickey's front stoop.

"Somebody die, Mr. Moriarty?" I asked.

"No, Danny. Just making my rounds."

Mr. Moriarty comes around several times a year and shakes everybody's hands so they will remember him "in their time of need."

"Any good wakes going on, Mr. Moriarty?"

Mr. Moriarty paused and lifted his black stovepipe hat and scratched under it with one finger.

"Well," he said, "there's Mr. Milke down on One-Hundred-First."

"Who's he?" I asked.

"Oh," said Mr. Moriarty, like he was about to tell me something very impressive. "Why, he was a taxidermist down at the Museum of Natural History."

"No kidding? What's a taxidermist?"

"A person who stuffs all the animals and birds for display."

"Wow," I said. "Even the tigers?"

Mr. Moriarty nodded. "Even the elephants."

"Wow," I said again. "What a neat job. What'd he die of?"

"Heart," said Mr. Moriarty, shaking his head sadly.

"That's too bad," I said.

"Indeed," said Mr. Moriarty, "indeed." He heaved a heavy sigh.

"Was he a friend of yours?" I asked.

"I like to think of all my customers as friends," said Mr. Moriarty. He sighed again.

I shook my head. "You sure must lose a lot of friends," I said.

Mr. Moriarty nodded sadly. "Well, good day, son," he said. "Remember me in your time of need." He reached his hand out to me and I shook it gingerly. It was cold and white, and it gave me the heebie-jeebies to think I was shaking the hand that touched all those dead bodies. He walked on down the steps, all stooped over and somber. I was still watching him when Mickey walked out the door.

"What're you looking at?" he asked.

"Mr. Moriarty."

"Why?"

I shook my head. "He sure is good at mourning," I said.

Mickey shrugged. "It's his job. What do you expect?"

I nodded. "I suppose. Hey, he said there's a good wake down on One-Hundred-First."

"Oh yeah? Who?"

"Some guy named Milke. Wanna go?"

"I thought you have to work."

"I got the day off. You wanna go or not?"

"I dunno," said Mickey. "I told Kitty I'd come by."

"Jeez, again?"

"What d'ya mean *again?*"

"You just saw her yesterday."

"So?"

"And the day before, and the day before that."

"So?"

"So what about you and me, Mick? We don't hardly do nothing together anymore."

"We played stickball yesterday."

"Oh wow, for all of an hour, 'til *she* came along."

Mickey looked torn for a moment, then we heard a door bang shut and looked over to see Maggie and Kitty standing on their stoop. Mickey's face lit up like a streetlamp.

"I know," he said, "we'll all go."

He ran over and grabbed Kitty's hand and pulled her down the steps. "C'mon," he said, "we're going to a wake." He looked back at me. "Well," he said. "What are you waiting for?"

"Nothin'," I grumbled. I shoved my hands in my pockets and walked on over. Maggie still stood on the stoop.

"You coming?" Mickey asked her.

She shrugged and looked at me. I looked down at the sidewalk and kicked at a loose chunk of cement.

"C'mon, you two," Mickey pleaded, "it's a wake."

"Please, Maggie," Kitty's soft voice added.

I looked up. Maggie smiled and came down the steps.

"Sure," she said. "There's nothing I like better than a good wake."

Mickey and Kitty skipped off together like little kids and left the two of us standing there.

"Well," said Maggie, "it looks like it's just you and me again, Wild Bill."

I smiled and drew an imaginary six-gun from my hip and aimed it at Mickey's back. Maggie drew one too and aimed it at Kitty.

"Bang! Bang!" we shouted.

Mickey and Kitty glanced disgustedly over their shoulders at us like we were hopelessly childish.

Maggie sighed. "Kitty sure has changed," she said.

I nodded. "Yeah, Mickey too."

We holstered our guns and walked on in silence. Maggie looked at me after a while, and I looked back, then we both looked away. There didn't seem to be anything else to say. I felt my ears starting to burn. Why is it so hard to talk to her all of a sudden? We've been friends all our lives. I looked at Mickey and Kitty giggling up ahead. It was all their fault somehow. Why did they have to fall in love and change everything?

"So how come you're not at the store today?" asked Maggie at last.

"Weissman gave me the day off."

"How come?"

"I dunno. I guess he was in a real good mood about the election."

Maggie smiled. "Yeah," she said. "I guess everybody is."

We walked on again in silence.

"How's your ma doing?" Maggie asked suddenly.

I looked at her. "Fine. Why?"

"I heard her in the toilet, throwing up again this morning. Is she expecting another baby?"

My stomach twisted into a sharp, painful knot, and for a moment I couldn't seem to catch my breath.

"No," I said hoarsely. "She's got a touch of the flu is all. Caught it from Mrs. Mahoney."

Maggie stared at me and I stared back at her, wanting desperately for her to believe what I'd just said so I could go on believing it. At last she nodded and I was able to breathe again.

TWENTY-THREE

When we got to 101st we looked for the funeral wreath. It was on a building on the other side of the street, up toward Madison Avenue. It was a nice building with fancy iron railings and front steps that came down to a landing and then curved down on both the right and the left to the street. There were potted plants on the landing, and the funeral wreath was big and full, tied with a pink ribbon, which means Mr. Milke wasn't too old. When it's an old person, the ribbon is purple, and when it's a kid, it's white. Ma always gets all teary-eyed when she sees a building with a white funeral wreath on it.

We caught up with Mickey and Kitty at the foot of the stairs.

"Looks like a rich one," Mickey said. "Who'd you say he was?"

"Mr. Milke," I told him, "a taxidermist from down at the Museum of Natural History."

Mickey looked puzzled, but he glanced at Kitty and Maggie and didn't say anything more. We all brushed ourselves off and tucked ourselves in, and spit on our shoes and wiped them with our sleeves. Mickey passed around an onion he'd grabbed off a vegetable cart on the way over. We all squeezed it and sniffed until our eyes got red and watery.

"All set?" asked Mickey.

The rest of us nodded.

"Okay," said Mickey, "follow me."

The hallway inside was dark and fancy, with polished marble floors and fine woodwork. I tapped Mickey on the shoulder.

"I don't know, Mick," I whispered. "Maybe it's too fancy."

Mickey waved my words away. "Don't be silly," he said. "It's just an apartment building. Believe me. Guys like him don't make that much money, no matter what kind of highfalutin names they call themselves."

"Okay," I said. Mickey started up the stairs and the rest of us followed. The wake was all the way up on the fourth floor. The apartments were set up like ours, with the kitchen door toward the back of the building and the living-room door toward the front. There was no toilet in the hall, though, so I guess each apartment had its own.

There were a few people standing out in the hall.

They were well dressed and looked down their noses at us as we filed by and went in through the front-room door. The casket was there, set up in front of the window and surrounded by more flowers than I'd ever seen in one place before. The air was heavy and sweet, and the room was full of red-eyed women dressed in black who sniffled and whispered to each other through rumpled handkerchiefs. All around, on the walls and tables and even standing on the floor, were stuffed birds and animals that stared at us with beady glass eyes.

The four of us worked our way over to the casket, where we went down on our knees and crossed ourselves. Mickey bent his head and whispered in my ear.

"What do you think all them dead animals are for?" he asked. "You think he's trying to take them with him like those Egyptian guys used to?"

"Quit foolin' around," I told him, trying not to laugh. "You're supposed to be saying a prayer." I crossed myself again.

"Dear Lord," I prayed, "please take this guy to heaven if he was good, and if he wasn't, please try not to be too tough on him. It's probably hard for you to understand, being God and all, but for us people it's not easy to be good *all* the time. Thank you, Lord. Amen."

One by one we got to our feet and stood staring down into the casket. Mr. Milke reminded me of one of his stuffed animals, except that his skin looked like it was carved out of pale pink wax. He had thinnish black hair combed low on his forehead, not a strand out of place, and a handlebar moustache that curled up so stiffly it looked like it would break off if you touched it. His face was all powdered up, and circles of rouge stained his cheeks. Black pencil outlined his lids and brows, and purplish lipstick colored his mouth.

"Doesn't he look natural?" I said.

The others nodded and murmured in agreement.

I sighed and clasped my hands together and made my way over to the chief lady in black, who was seated on a chair on the other side of the casket.

"I'm very sorry, ma'am," I said.

The lady stopped dabbing at her eyes and looked up at me, then beyond me at the other three.

"Who are you?" she asked.

"We were friends with Mr. Milke down at the museum," I said.

She continued to stare at me, obviously unconvinced, when Maggie started sniffling. She was rubbing her eyes with her hand, the one she'd squeezed the onion with. Tears started streaming down her cheeks.

"He was such a good man," she blubbered, "always so kind to us kids."

That did the widow in. She started blubbering, too. "Oh yes," she said. "He did love children. We never had any of our own, you know."

"I know," I said gently. "He spoke of it often. It was a sorrow to him."

The woman sighed and nodded. "Yes, yes, to me,

too. Well, thank you so much for coming. Do be sure and go into the kitchen and have something to eat before you go. Herbert would never forgive me if you didn't."

"Yes, ma'am. Thank you, ma'am," we all murmured.

We walked solemnly over to the door, breathed a sigh of relief that the formalities were over, and beat it around back to the kitchen.

The kitchen was thick with smoke and crowded with men who were puffing on cigarettes and sipping bootleg whiskey, telling off-color jokes and trying not to laugh too loudly. They paid no attention to us as we swarmed around the table.

It was a great wake all right. They had baked ham and roast turkey, all kinds of cheeses, and big, hard rolls. There were pies and tarts and cookies and cakes and fruit. Our eyes were bugging out as we loaded up our plates and stuffed extras into our pockets and coats. Mickey was trying to shove a banana up his sleeve when the widow suddenly appeared at his shoulder.

"Are you getting enough to eat, children?" she asked.

We all nodded somberly.

She looked at Mickey. "It still puzzles me," she said, "how you came to know Mr. Milke at the museum. In his line of work he didn't get out front much."

Mickey shot me a puzzled glance, then looked back

at the widow. "We . . . uh . . . met him out back," he said.

"Out back?"

"Y-yeah," Mickey stuttered. "He . . . uh, used to take us for rides when he was off duty."

"Rides?"

"Yeah. You know, in his cab."

"Cab? Young man, there must be some mistake."

"No," said Mickey, turning red. "No mistake. He used to give us rides in his taxi cab . . ."

I was laughing so hard telling Mama the story that I was spitting beans all over the table.

"Daniel," said Mama, laughing too. "Please don't be talkin' with yer mouth full."

"Okay, okay," I said, putting my fork down. "So anyway, I told him a taxidermist is a guy who stuffs dead animals for museums." I started to laugh again. "So he says, 'How was I supposed to know? I thought it was some highfalutin name for a taxi driver.' "

I slid down in my chair, laughing 'til my sides ached and tears ran down my cheeks. Mama laughed, too, long and hard. Then suddenly she grew quiet and pale.

"Mama? You all right?"

"Aye, aye. I just need a sip of water, I think." She got up and walked unsteadily to the sink, where she put both hands on the rim and leaned heavily forward.

"Mama?"

She clutched her stomach with one hand, put the other over her mouth, and fled out into the hall.

Maureen began to cry and I picked her up out of her chair. She put her arms around my neck and we sat there, clinging to one another and listening to Mama retch.

TWENTY-FOUR

Wednesday, November 23, 1932

Thanksgiving Eve, and still no word from Pa. I felt angry and deserted as I swept up at the store. Surely he could have reached us somehow, if he really wanted to.

Mr. Weissman came over. He took hold of my hand, turned it palm up, and dropped something into it. "Happy Thanksgiving," he said.

I looked down. It was Pa's watch. "What's this for?" I asked.

"Your debt is paid," said Mr. Weissman. "Today is your last day at the store."

I stared at the watch. "But . . . it's only Thanksgiving, not Christmas," I argued. "Pa promised you . . ."

Mr. Weissman held up his hand for silence. He arched a bushy white brow. "Did you break the window?" he asked.

I shook my head slowly. "No."

Mr. Weissman gave a short nod, then a hint of a smile twitched at the corners of his mouth. "Happy Thanksgiving," he repeated.

I smiled. He was telling me he believed me.

"Thanks, Mr. Weissman," I said.

He nodded again and gave my shoulder a quick pat.

I held the watch up by the chain and looked at it.

"I'll bet this is really worth a lot of money, huh?" I said.

Mr. Weissman shrugged. "About two dollars."

"Two dollars!" I stared at him, openmouthed. He nodded and walked away. "Wait a minute," I said. "Oh, I get it. You're kidding me, right?"

Mr. Weissman turned and looked back at me. He wasn't laughing. "Your grandfather in Ireland . . . ," he said, "he was a wealthy man?"

"Well, no, but . . ."

"Two dollars," Mr. Weissman repeated, then walked away again.

I looked more closely at the watch. Mr. Weissman was right. Around the edges the shiny gold was wearing off and you could just start to see a dull gray metal showing through. I walked over to the counter where Mr. Weissman was finishing the day's tallies in the black book.

"I don't get it, Mr. Weissman," I said. "If you knew the watch wasn't valuable, why'd you make the deal?"

Mr. Weissman's bushy eyebrows lifted and he peered at me over the rims of his reading glasses.

"Valuable?" he said. "Who said it wasn't valuable?"

"But you said . . ."

"I said it was probably worth about two dollars. What has that to do with value? *This* . . . this is value."

Mr. Weissman grabbed the watch from my hand, opened it up, and pointed to the inscription. I looked again at the words Pa had shown me many times:

JUNE 16, 1917

GOD BLESS YOU MY SON

D. T. G.

Daniel Tomas Garvey—my grandfather. My eyes misted up for a minute and I looked down and blinked them clear so Mr. Weissman wouldn't see.

"No money can buy that kind of value," said Mr. Weissman, closing the watch and handing it back to me. "Now go, and tell your mother happy Thanksgiving."

"Mr. Weissman," I said, when my voice steadied, "I was just thinking. . . ."

Mr. Weissman peered over his rims and waited for me to go on.

"Well, I mean, I was wondering if maybe you could still use some help here. You wouldn't have to pay me much. Whatever you think I'm worth would be . . . fine. . . ."

Mr. Weissman had closed the big black book and stood staring down at it. He sucked in a large breath that expanded his chest, then he let it out slowly and shook his head.

"It's not that I don't need the help, Danny," he said, looking up at last.

I met his eyes, then looked away. They were so sad.

"And it's not that you're not a good worker. . . ." He rubbed his hand over the black book, picked it up as if it were very heavy, and slid it under the counter. "It's just that . . ."

"I know, Mr. Weissman. Thanks anyhow."

Mr. Weissman nodded. I reached out my hand to him and he took it and clasped it warmly in his.

"Your papa was right," he said. "You're a good boy, Danny."

I smiled. "Wish he could hear you say that," I said.

"I'll tell him, soon as he gets back."

"Thanks, Mr. Weissman."

I turned and headed for the door, then stopped suddenly and turned back.

"Hey, Mr. Weissman. What d'ya say I check back with you about that job next summer, when the depression's over?"

Mr. Weissman laughed and shook his head.

"You do that, Danny," he said.

TWENTY-FIVE

The whole building smelled like pies and cakes and good things to eat when I got home. Kitchen doors were open and people bustled back and forth, borrowing this and that, and sharing sips of holiday cheer. Over all I could hear Mama singing. My heart leapt at the sound. Her song was full of joy, and that could mean but one thing—Pa!

I bounded up the stairs and burst into the kitchen. Ma turned from the stove, her face all lit up with smiles, and reached her arms out to me. I rushed into them.

"Is Pa home?" I asked.

"No," she said, laughing, "but look what came today."

She pulled an envelope from her apron pocket and I snatched it before she could say another word. Some money fluttered from the envelope as I pulled the letter free, but I didn't even stop to pick it up. I unfolded the paper and feasted my eyes on Pa's messy handwriting. Misspellings and all, it looked beautiful to me. I wanted to hug the paper, but I guessed Ma would think I was pretty silly, so I sat down at the table and read:

My dearest Molly,

I'm sorry not to have wrote before this, but stamps and paper are hard to come by. I found a few days work fixing up a burnt down barn but nothing stedy yet. I'll not be home for Thanksgiving darlin, but if you take this money and have a fine feast I will share it with you in my heart. There's word of some mill-work farther up the coast, so I'll be moving on tonite.

Molly my love I'll do all in my power to be home with you on Christmas, and I will count the days till then. Give my love to Danny and Maureen. Till Christmas I am

Your devoted,
Daniel

I swallowed my disappointment over Pa's not being able to make it for Thanksgiving, and clung to his promise of being home for Christmas. I grabbed the envelope and looked at the postmark: New London, Connecticut.

"Ma, where's New London, Connecticut?"

Mama pulled our worn old copy of the map of the United States from her pocket. She'd already looked it up.

"I'm not positive," she said, "but Mrs. Mahoney is thinkin' it's right about here."

She pointed to a spot about two thirds of the way up the coast of Connecticut. It was only about a half an inch from New York.

"That's not so far," I said.

Mama smiled and shook her head.

"And he'll be home for Christmas."

Mama smiled and nodded.

"Can't you talk?" I asked her.

"No," said Mama. "I'm so glad to hear from him, I'm too happy for talkin'."

She took Pa's letter and hugged it to her chest. I laughed.

"I wanted to do that, too," I said, "but I thought you'd laugh."

"And what's wrong with laughin'?" said Mama. She handed me the letter and I hugged it tight, then we laughed and hugged each other. Maureen toddled over and tugged at my knee. We scooped her up and hugged her, too.

My head was still filled with happiness when I went to bed. I lay awake, dreaming of all the good things ahead. Tomorrow is Thanksgiving. In the morning us kids will dress like ragamuffins like we do every Thanksgiving, and go door to door begging pennies. Usually I get to keep whatever I collect and buy candy, but this year I'm planning to give it all to Ma, and just save out a little to buy Pa a Christmas present.

After we're done collecting tomorrow, we'll go over to Lexington Avenue and watch the Macy's parade like we always do. Then we'll come home to a big dinner at the Rileys'. The only way it could be better would be if Pa were here. But he'll be home for Christmas. . . . He'll be home for Christmas. . . . He'll be home for Christmas. . . .

TWENTY-SIX

The sound woke me from a deep sleep, but I knew instantly what it was, and I sat up, shaking. Mama appeared in the doorway, pulling on her robe.

"They're coming this way," I whispered.

"Aye," said Mama.

"Can we go see?"

"All right then, but wrap up in your blanket."

We went into the front room, crouched down, and approached the window cautiously. We pulled the curtain aside and peeked out. They came careening up from downtown—three big black limousines. The car in front swerved from curb to curb, trying to get away from the two behind, but they were closing fast. Machine-gun fire lit up the night, and as they passed our building we ducked and listened to the *ping, ping, ping* of the bullets bouncing off the bricks.

When the noise died away we looked out again

and watched them disappear into the darkness uptown. A shrill scream shattered the newly restored quiet, and a police car sped by, then another, and another. Just as it grew quiet again, the elevated train rumbled by, its few late-night passengers, their noses pressed to the window, still straining to see the commotion in the street below.

Mama put an arm around me and I could feel that she was trembling, too. I lifted my blanket and pulled it around us both.

"Bloody bootleggers," Mama whispered. "If they want to kill each other, why can't they go far out in the country, where innocent folks aren't likely to get in their way?"

I stared at her, shocked to hear such a word from her mouth.

"I'm sorry," she said. "I shouldn't speak so, but I'm just so tired of these hoodlums and their gangland wars, fighting over who has the right to peddle their bootleg whiskey and where."

"It'll be over soon," I said, "if Roosevelt ends Prohibition like he promised."

"Aye, let's hope so," said Mama. "It's been a long time since the streets were safe for decent people."

She looked at me and smiled a little. "We're a fine pair, aren't we," she said. "One of us shakin' worse than the other. It's not like it never happened before."

"No," I said, "but Pa was always here."

Mama sighed and nodded. She stared out the window into the night. "I know," she said. "When I was a child on the farm, there was never food enough to last the winter. My daddy would go over the water to England and work to get us through. Things were never quite right when he was gone. Scary things were scarier; lonely times were lonelier. We were like a wagon with one wheel missing, and no matter what the rest of us did, we couldna' get that wagon to ride smooth."

I looked at Mama and my heart filled with love for her. She isn't like other grown-ups. She remembers how it feels to be a kid. Times like this she can look back inside herself and feel just what I'm feeling and understand. It's a comfort to know that. I wanted to tell her how I felt. *I love you, Mama.* It used to be so easy to say when I was little. But now that I'm older, it always seems to stick in my throat.

"Come now," Mama said, getting stiffly to her feet. "The excitement is over. They've probably shot each other to pieces by now. I'm just hoping there weren't any innocents in the way."

I got up and pulled the blanket tight around me.

"Can us kids go up and look for blood on the sidewalk in the morning?" I asked.

Mama grimaced and gave me a playful swat on the rear.

"Go on with you!"

"Aw c'mon, Ma."

"Never you mind. Such thoughts! Into bed with you now."

Ma tucked me in, then stood for a moment smiling down at me. I saw her slide her hand gently across her stomach the way she always did when she was expecting. Knowing now that Pa was coming home, I found the courage to ask her.

"Ma, are you expecting again?"

Even in the semidarkness I could see the deep flush that spread across her face.

"Danny . . . such a question!"

"Mama, I'm not a kid anymore. I know what it's all about."

She smiled a little. "Do ya now?"

"Yes, I do."

"Then maybe *you* should be tellin' me."

"C'mon, Ma."

She laughed. "All right then. I am, Mr. Know-it-all. You'll be havin' a new brother or sister come the end of May."

"But Mama, the doctor said you weren't to have any more."

"And who told you that?"

"I overheard."

"You're overhearin' a lot lately, aren't you?"

"Mama, please answer me."

"Answer you what?"

"Did you know when Pa left?"

"I . . . wasn't sure."

"But you suspected."

"Aye."

"Then why didn't you tell him? He never would've left if he'da known."

Mama frowned. "What would you have me tell

162

him, Danny? That there's to be another mouth to add to those he can't feed already?"

"But he would have *stayed,* Ma."

"Aye." Mama slumped down onto the bed beside me and rubbed her eyes tiredly with her hands. She looked at me. "I wanted to tell him," she said. "I almost did, but I couldn't. If I'da made him stay, he would've died."

"Died?"

"Aye. Haven't you seen them on the stoops and the street corners—men forced to stand idle while their families go hungry? Men with strong backs and clever minds, asking only for work, getting handouts instead. After a while they get that empty look in their eyes that means they've no hope left, no pride. I've seen them a million times, back home and now here—dead men walking around. I couldn't stand to see yer pa like that."

I knew she was right, but I didn't care. I'm tired of acting grown-up and trying to be a man. I just want Pa to come home and stay home and take care of things like he always did, so I can be a kid again.

TWENTY-SEVEN

Saturday, December 24, 1932

There's no place in the world like New York at Christmastime. Mama laughs when I say that and says, how would I know? But I do know. Where else can you smell fresh-cut Christmas trees and hot-roasted chestnuts on the same street corner? Where else can you take the subway downtown for a nickel and spend the whole day looking in shop windows at electric trains and wind-up cars and model boats and planes— treasures you can never hope to own, but it doesn't matter, because it's glory enough just to look at them? And where else would everyone on the street smile and wish you "Merry Christmas!" even in the middle of the depression, when hardly anyone has very much to be merry about?

Today is Christmas Eve! We haven't heard from Pa yet, but I'm not worried. There's still time, and besides, it would be just like Pa to pop up and surprise us without writing ahead. I suspect he'll show up any minute now.

My idea about saving the money I'd collected on Thanksgiving didn't pan out. I didn't collect any. Not a single cent. Folks just didn't have any money to spare, I guess. "Sorry," everyone said, "maybe next year." So I saved a little out of my shoeshine money each week, and now I have sixty cents. Not a fortune, but it'll have to do. I've had my eye on a pound box of Fanny Farmer chocolates down at Mr. Weissman's. Pa has a real sweet tooth. It costs a whole dollar, though, and even if I could come up with another forty cents, which I can't, that would still leave nothing over for Ma and Maureen. I decided instead to go on over to the five-and-dime after I've dropped off the linens, and see what I can find.

Sadie was smiling wider than ever when she let me in the back door of Miss Emily's.

"Merry Christmas, merry Christmas!" she cried, looking for all the world like a jolly, chocolate Mrs. Claus.

"Merry Christmas, Sadie," I told her.

She pushed a heaping tray of Christmas cookies at me.

"No thanks, Sadie," I said, backing away.

"Oh g'wan," said Sadie. "It's Christmas!" Then she winked and added under her breath, "Even *herself* has a heart at Christmas."

I took a cookie and nodded my thanks.

"I'll tell her you're here," said Sadie, bustling out

of the kitchen. A few minutes later she pushed the swinging door open and motioned for me to come in.

I made a face.

"C'mon," she whispered, winking to let me know it was okay.

We walked through the fancy dining room and out into the front room. It was big and dark with a huge, high ceiling and heavy green velvet drapes that hung all the way to the floor, blocking out any hint of sunshine. Miss Emily sat at a small writing desk in the corner, her back to us. Sadie gave me a push in her direction. I pulled off my cap and walked over to the desk. Miss Emily went on writing as if I wasn't there. I looked back at Sadie, but she was gone. I stood like that a few minutes more, shifting from one foot to the other and twisting my cap in my hands.

"You needn't fidget so," said Miss Emily, taking me by surprise and making me jump. I planted my feet flat on the floor and willed my hands to stay still by my sides. A few more minutes went by in which I had every itch and twitch imaginable, but somehow I managed to stay still.

At last Miss Emily finished her writing, placed her pen to one side, and picked up a small purse. Without a word she opened it, counted out ten dollar bills, and snapped it shut. Then, like an afterthought, she opened it again and took out one more dollar.

"Merry Christmas," she said, pushing the bills at me across the desk without ever looking up. She took up her pen again and went back to her writing.

I picked up the ten and left the one on the desk. "Mama don't let me take charity," I said.

At that Miss Emily tilted her head up and scowled at me.

"Don't be absurd, young man," she said, picking up the last dollar and shoving it into my hand. "A Christmas tip is not charity. Now, go."

Sadie had reappeared in the doorway and was gesturing madly for me to come.

"Th-thank you, ma'am," I stammered to Miss Emily. "Merry Christmas to you, too."

"Don't you be lookin' no gift horse in the mouth," Sadie told me when she got me back out into the kitchen. "Your mama worked hard all year and she deserves that tip."

"Yes, ma'am."

"Don't you 'ma'am' me. You run along home now and y'all have a Merry Christmas, you hear?"

"You, too, Sadie."

Once I got back out on the street and over the shock, it suddenly occurred to me that thanks to Miss Emily I now had enough money to buy Pa that box of chocolates. I had a little bit of a fight with my conscience over the fact that it really was Mama's tip and I had no right to spend it. But the more I kept picturing Pa opening that box of candy on Christmas morning, the quieter my conscience got, until the next thing I knew, I was walking into Mr. Weissman's store.

I picked out a pound of Fanny Farmer and plunked it down on the counter with the dollar bill on top. Mr. Weissman looked up at me and arched his eyebrows in surprise.

"It's a Christmas present," I told him proudly. "Pa is coming home."

"Ah." Mr. Weissman smiled. "A special occasion indeed." He took the dollar, rang the cash register, and handed me two quarters back.

"What's this for?" I asked.

"A sale," said Mr. Weissman. "I'm running a sale."

"No kidding?" I started to grin over my good fortune, when suddenly I realized what Mr. Weissman was doing. "Oh no," I said, pushing the quarters back across the counter. "I'm payin' for this fair and square."

"What? What do you mean?" Mr. Weissman started to bluster, but I just scooped up the candy and dashed out the door. "Merry Christmas, Mr. Weissman!" I shouted over my shoulder.

After that I stopped into the five-and-dime and picked out a tube of Flame-Glo lipstick for Ma. It's a real pretty purply color, and I was sure she'd love it. For Maureen I decided on a big string of wooden beads. That left a nickel over, so I bought some red wrapping paper with Santa faces all over it. Walking home with my secrets tucked under my arm, I thought that if Christmas didn't hurry up and come I was sure to explode.

Mama looked disappointed when I handed her the ten dollars and mumbled something under her breath about an old skinflint. I realized with a pang of guilt that she'd been expecting that tip, probably even planning on it. I thought for a second of telling her what I'd done, but I so much wanted to surprise everyone.

"I fear it's goin' to be a bit of a lean Christmas this year, Danny," Ma said.

"I don't care," I told her, and I don't. As long as Pa comes home, I don't need any other presents. Ma still looked disappointed, but I eased my conscience by telling myself that she only would've spent the money on me anyway, and I'd much rather have it spent on Pa.

"Well, we'll be havin' a tree at least," said Ma, separating one of the bills from the others.

"Now?" I asked. "Can we go now?" Getting the tree, to me, is almost as exciting as Christmas morning itself.

Mama smiled and nodded.

I dragged Mama and Maureen halfway across New York, from corner to corner to corner. The tree had to be just right for Pa's welcome home, and I couldn't be sure until I'd seen them all. Satisfied at last that I'd seen every tree within walking distance, I decided on one of the first ones we'd looked at, right on our own street corner. Ma pretended to be annoyed, but I knew she really wasn't. When it comes to Christmas she's a bigger kid than I am.

TWENTY-EIGHT

There was still no sign of Pa when we got home. I could tell by Ma's face that she was growing nervous.

"Don't worry," I told her, "he'll be here."

She nodded, but she didn't look convinced.

"Maybe he called," I said. "I'll run down to the candy store and see." The candy store has the only phone in the neighborhood.

"Mrs. DeLuca would've sent word," Mama said.

"Maybe she tried to while we were out."

"All right," Mama said, "run and see then, if it'll make you feel any better."

Mrs. DeLuca had about twenty customers in the store and she seemed flustered and out of sorts.

"Phone calls?" she snapped. "Of course there's been phone calls. Fool thing's been ringin' off the hook all day. I've half a mind to yank it out."

As if to prove what she'd said, the phone started ringing. Mrs. DeLuca just shook her head and went on helping her customer.

"I'll get it for you," I told her. I went around behind the counter, my heart leaping with every ring of the phone. I put the receiver to my ear and stretched up to reach the mouthpiece.

"Hello!" I shouted over the noise of the crowd.

"Hello . . . hello," came the operator's tinny voice. "I have a long distance call for—"

There was a burst of static and I couldn't hear what she'd said.

"For who?" I shouted.

"Mrs. Clark," said the operator. "Is there a Mrs. Clark there?"

"Oh," I said, my heart sinking. "Just a minute, I'll see." I turned to the crowd. "Is there a Mrs. Clark here?" I shouted.

"Oh yes, yes!"

A little gray-haired woman in a polka-dotted housedress detached herself from the opposite wall and hurried over. "It's my daughter," she told me, her eyes shining as she took the receiver, "all the way from California. I've been waiting all day for her call."

"That's nice," I managed to tell her.

I looked over at Mrs. DeLuca. I guess I must've looked as disappointed as I felt, because her grumpy scowl softened. She excused herself to her customer and came over to me.

"Look, Danny," she said, "if your papa calls I'll

get word to you, okay? Even if he calls tonight or tomorrow I'll run downstairs here and answer. Now cheer up, all right? It's Christmas."

"Okay, thanks, Mrs. DeLuca."

"Here," she said, taking a candy cane out of a jar, "a present."

"Thanks, Mrs. DeLuca, but I'm not too hungry."

"Hang it on your tree then, and tell your mama I said Merry Christmas."

"Thank you. Merry Christmas to you, too, Mrs. DeLuca."

When I got back to our building, the whole Riley gang was filing out the front door. They looked like a bunch of ragamuffins, one shabbier than the other.

"What're you all dressed up for?" I asked. "It's Christmas, not Thanksgiving."

Maggie gave me a wink. "The Ladies' Aid Society is giving away Christmas baskets over at the park," she said. "The worse you look, the sorrier they feel, and the more they give you."

"Well, you oughta get the whole load then."

Maggie stuck out her tongue. "Wouldn't hurt you none to come along," she said. "Your ma could do with a little extra, same as mine."

"That's charity," I told her. "We don't take charity."

Maggie's face flushed red when I said that, and her eyes gave off angry little sparks. "Oh? Is that so, Mr. High-and-Mighty? And I suppose that you'll be just too high and mighty to eat it once we've brung it home, too, won't you?"

That made me squirm some. After all, we were going to the Rileys' for Christmas dinner. I was still trying to come up with an answer when Maggie turned and stomped away.

"Men!" she shouted over her shoulder. "You're all the same—useless!"

The other Rileys followed after her. Little Johnny looked at me questioningly as he went by. His Jack Armstrong ring was on his finger.

"Oh, all right, I'm coming," I shouted. I shoved my hands into my pockets and scuffed along after them. Maggie ignored me 'til we got to the park, then she turned on me again.

"What are *you* following us for?"

I shrugged and kicked at the grass. "I . . . uh . . . figure you're right," I mumbled. "My ma could do with a little extra, same as yours."

"Well, I'll be," said Maggie. "Is that an apology?"

I shrugged again. "I guess so, if you wanna take it that way."

The fire went out of Maggie's eyes. She never was one to hold a grudge. "Look, Danny," she said. "There isn't any shame in it. Our mothers work hard. So do we. It's not our fault the way things are."

I swallowed down the lump that was forming in my throat and tore at a tuft of brown grass with the toe of my shoe. "I s'pose," I said. "What do we have to do?"

"Just follow me. It's not so bad."

I followed the Rileys over to a large platform. A table had been set up on the platform, and four rich-looking ladies in fur coats and fancy hats sat behind it. To their left were stacked hundreds of food baskets tied with bright red ribbons. A crowd of people lined up below, to the right of the platform. A few at a time they went up onto the platform, paused a moment in front of the furry ladies, got their baskets, and went down the other side. As our turn got closer, I could see that the ladies were questioning each of the people and scribbling down notes on pieces of paper.

"What are they asking?" I whispered to Maggie.

"They ask you a few questions, that's all, to see if you really deserve a basket."

"What?"

"Shh! Just answer them. It's no big deal."

It was Maggie's turn, and she and Kitty herded all the little Rileys up onto the stage. They sure looked a sight. I could see the rich ladies stealing pitying glances at one another.

"Where are your parents?" one of the ladies demanded.

Maggie took a step forward. "Our mother is working," she said. "She's a janitor."

"And your father?"

"He's . . . in jail."

"For what reason?" another lady asked.

Maggie looked down at the platform floor and mumbled something.

"Louder, please," the woman said.

"Beating us," Maggie replied, her face bright red.

The women looked at each other and shook their heads.

"Very well then," the first one said. "Move along. Give two baskets to these children," she called over to one of the helpers.

"Thank you all," I heard Maggie say, "and merry Christmas."

I hated it. I hated the whole thing. I wanted to turn and run, but I couldn't. I was already halfway up the platform steps, and the crowd behind was pushing me along.

"Next," one of the women called.

I stepped forward. Four pairs of eyes looked me up and down.

"And where are your parents, young man?" the first lady asked.

"My pa went to look for work," I said.

"Where?"

"I . . . don't know."

The woman nodded as if to say she'd expected as much.

"And your mother?"

"She's home."

"Does she work?"

"She takes in ironing."

"Have you any brothers and sisters?"

"A baby sister, and . . ."

"And what?"

"And another on the way."

One of the other women looked up sharply. "How long has your father been gone?" she asked.

I stared at her. "Not that long," I said.

She narrowed her eyes and looked back at her paper.

"All right," said the first woman. "Take your basket and move along."

The woman who handed me the basket had kind eyes. "Merry Christmas," she said, smiling. My face burned as I took it from her.

"We ain't really poor," I told her. "My pa's coming home again, and everything's gonna be fine."

"I'm glad," she said.

TWENTY-NINE

<figure>ornamental divider</figure>

Christmas Day, 1932

As soon as I opened my eyes, I slid from my bed and crept over to the doorway. I pulled the curtain aside, praying that during the night, while I'd slept, another lump had appeared in Mama's bed. There was only one. She rolled over and looked at me.

"Merry Christmas," she said.

"Merry Christmas," I answered quietly.

Mama sat up in bed.

"Come here, Danny," she said, patting the mattress beside her. She reached for her apron, hanging on the bedpost, and took a ragged piece of paper from the pocket. I recognized it as Pa's letter. She opened it and put it into my hand.

"There," she said. "Read that line."

I read: "Molly, my love, I'll do all in my power to be home with you on Christmas, and—"

"That'll be enough," Mama interrupted. "Do you

see what it says there, Danny? *In my power.* Some things are not within our power. Pa may not be able to get home, and I don't want it to ruin your Christmas. He'll come when he can."

"No," I said, trying to keep the tears from my eyes. "He would've written. He would've called. He wouldn't just not show up—not on Christmas. He'll be here. I know he will."

A tear escaped from my eye and Ma reached out for me, but I twisted away from her.

"All right, all right," she said. "We'll wait and see then, just try not to be too disappointed if . . ."

Maureen woke up then and yelled to get out of her crib, and I was glad. I didn't want to hear Mama's words. They didn't fit into my plans.

We got cleaned up and dressed, and before long the whole Riley clan came charging over. They couldn't afford a tree of their own, so we'd left a note for Santa to leave their gifts under ours this year.

Mama and Mrs. Riley went into the front room first, and Maggie, Kitty, and I tried to keep the little ones from bursting with excitement while we waited for the candles to be lit.

"Did he come? Did he come?" they kept shouting.

At last Mama pulled the curtain aside.

"See for yourselves," she said.

Like a great wave, we surged through the door. The little ones threw themselves on the packages right away, but us older ones hung back a bit, just taking it all in. Outside the window, the morning was gloomy and damp, making the brightly burning candles seem all the cheerier. Mama had lit the kerosene stove for the occasion, so the room was warm and pleasant, too. The tree, we agreed, was the best ever. With its popcorn chains and cotton balls, cranberry ropes and handmade ornaments, it was far more elegant than the gaudy ones downtown.

Mama and Mrs. Riley waded among the little ones, oohing and ahing, and trying to maintain some sense of order. I looked at Mama. It has been a while since she's been sick in the mornings. She's thin, but her cheeks are pink, and aside from the way the buttons of her sweater pull tight across her middle, she looks perfectly normal.

I let myself forget for a moment that Ma's pregnant, that Pa's not home, and I melted into the joy of Christmas.

When the little ones had opened all their gifts and were playing with an assortment of tops, marbles, balls, jacks, and shoe-box doll carriages, I handed out my gifts. Mama loved her lipstick and said she would save it for special occasions. Maureen shook her beads up and down and put them in her mouth, so I guess she liked them, too.

"Who's that one for?" asked Maggie, pointing to Pa's unopened gift.

"Pa."

"Oh." She sounded disappointed.

"What's wrong?"

"Nothing." She produced a small, rectangular package from behind her back. "Here," she said, "this is for you."

My ears started to burn. "For me?"

"Yeah. Don't worry if you didn't get me anything. I don't care."

"No . . . no," I lied. "I got you something. See, it's right here." I groped around under the Christmas tree, pretending I was looking for something. "Gee, I must've dropped it when I was carrying everything in. I'll be right back."

I rushed through the spare room and into my bedroom and stood there chewing on my thumbnail. What on earth could I give her? I pulled my dresser drawer open and rummaged through, then I spied my treasure box. That gave me an idea. It wasn't much, but it was better than nothing. I found a scrap of paper in the wastebasket, wrapped my gift, and dashed back out into the front room.

"See," I said, handing it to her. "It's so small I didn't even realize I'd dropped it."

Maggie stared skeptically at the little lump in her hand.

"Took you long enough to find it," she said.

"Yeah. Well . . . it . . . uh . . . rolled under the dresser!"

"Oh."

"So, open it."

"You open yours first."

"All right, let's open them together," I said. I tore my paper off. *Black Beauty!* No kidding? Where'd you get it?" It was a worn copy, and the binding was taped, but I was thrilled to own it.

Maggie shrugged. "Just around," she said. "I knew

it was your favorite." She finished peeling the wrapper off of hers. She smiled. "Your Tom Mix branding iron."

"Yeah. I knew you always wanted one."

She laughed and nodded. She lifted the rubber stamp from its inkpad and looked at it. Then she gave me a funny sidelong glance, and the next thing I knew, I was branded, right in the middle of my forehead.

Everybody burst out laughing. "Look," Johnny shouted. "Danny belongs to Maggie now."

THIRTY

I thought Pa might meet us at church and surprise us. I stared back at the doors all during Mass, but he never came in. Then I hoped he'd be waiting for us by the time we got back home. But he wasn't.

My heart must have stopped a hundred times during the day—every time the front door banged downstairs, every time footsteps thudded through the hall. Finally, while we were at dinner, some heavy footsteps thumped up the stairs and stopped outside of Rileys' door. There was a knock.

I looked at Mama, my heart jumping nearly out of my chest. She tried not to act excited, but her cheeks flushed bright red and it seemed that she, too, could hardly catch her breath.

"Come in," called Maggie's mother. "It's open."

I watched the doorknob turn and the door swing

open so slowly, almost like in a dream, and there, at last, stood . . . Mr. Riley.

I swallowed hard and shoved a big forkful of turkey into my mouth, trying to hide my disappointment. Maggie's mother stiffened in her chair.

"What do you want, John?" she asked tensely.

Mr. Riley stepped unsteadily into the room. A bag of oranges swung from his hand. "I brought the children a Chrizmuz prezent," he said, his words thick and slurred. He lifted the oranges higher.

"When did they let you out?" Maggie's mother asked.

"Las' week." Mr. Riley took another step into the room.

"Maggie," said Mrs. Riley, "please take the oranges from your father."

Maggie pushed her chair back from the table, then went around and took the sack her father held out. He turned his attention to her.

"Hello, baby," he said, reaching out to touch her cheek. The gesture seemed to throw him off balance and he lurched forward suddenly and grabbed Maggie around the shoulders to keep from falling.

Maggie waited for him to steady himself, then she twisted away and went over to put the oranges in the sink. She stood for a moment with her back to all of us, then suddenly she covered her face with her hands and fled back into the bedrooms. A strained silence settled over the table.

Mrs. Riley cleared her throat. "Thank you for the oranges, John," she said. "Good-bye."

Maggie's father made no move to leave. He took another step into the room. "I thought maybe . . ."

"Good-bye, John," Mrs. Riley repeated.

Maggie's father looked around the table. "Kitty," he said, "why don't you talk to yer ma?"

Mrs. Riley abruptly stood up. "Don't do this, John," she said, her voice trembling. "Don't ruin their Christmas."

Mr. Riley stared at her for a long moment, breathing loudly and swaying ever so slightly on his feet. At last he lowered his head, turned away, and shuffled silently out the door.

Mrs. Riley slumped down onto her chair and put her face into her hands. Kitty got up and went over to comfort her. I looked at Mama.

"I'll go see about Maggie," I said.

She nodded.

I walked through to Rileys' front room. It was rainy and dark, and Maggie's figure stood silhouetted against the window. She had pulled the thin curtain aside, but she let it fall as I came up behind her. In the gray light I could see tears shining on her cheek. Dimly, through the curtain, I saw Mr. Riley weave his way up the street and disappear into the 107th Street tunnel. Maggie's gaze followed him.

I swallowed hard, searching for something to say. "You want to talk about it?" I asked at last.

Maggie shook her head. "There's nothing to say."

I shoved my hands into my pockets and stood there, looking around awkwardly. Maggie didn't move. "You . . . uh, want me to leave?" I asked.

"No." Maggie turned and looked at me. Her eyes were wet and shining. "He used to hold me," she said, so softly I could hardly hear. "Ma was always busy with babies, but Pa used to hold me." Her bottom lip quivered and fresh tears slid down her cheeks.

Before I even realized what I was doing, I reached out and pulled her into my arms. She laid her head on my shoulder and sobbed. She must have been hurting bad to cry like that. Maggie doesn't cry easy. I felt a tenderness toward her that I'd never felt before.

After a while, her sobs died away, but she seemed content to stay with her head resting on my shoulder, and I was content to let her. It felt good to hold her, warm and close. She smelled like soap and fresh air, and her hair was soft against my cheek. I realized suddenly that we were standing shoulder to shoulder. I was as tall as she was now. When had that happened? Ma must be right. I *was* growing like a weed.

When at last she pulled away, Maggie kissed me lightly on the cheek, and I felt my face get hot and red.

"Thanks, Danny," she whispered.

"For what?"

"For being here."

THIRTY-ONE

Monday, January 2, 1933

Christmas vacation passed with never a word from Pa, and each day the weight in my chest grew heavier. Ma and I would surprise each other repeatedly at the front-room window, and we'd make lame excuses about what we were watching for, neither of us wanting to let on how worried we are. Mama is growing pale again, and I know the weight in her chest must be taking its toll, too.

Yesterday was New Year's Day and Ma wanted to take the tree down. But I wouldn't let her. We had worked so hard to pick it out; I couldn't bear to think that Pa wouldn't see it at all. When I left for school this morning, I made her promise that she wouldn't touch it. When I came home, it was gone.

"But you promised!" I yelled.

"What choice did I have?" Mama argued. "You wouldn't have left for school otherwise."

"You still broke your promise."

"And would you rather your father came home to find the whole buildin' burnt to the ground?"

"I don't care," I shouted. "I don't care!"

My eyes fell on the still wrapped box of chocolates sitting on the coffee table. I picked it up and hurled it across the room. It smashed against the wall, splitting open and spilling chocolates all over the floor.

"Danny!" Mama shouted. "That'll be enough. You go straight to your room and . . ."

I never heard the rest. I ran out into the hall, slammed the door behind me, and bolted down the stairs and out into the street.

It was snowing. It had been all day. The first snowstorm of the season. Normally I would have been as excited as a little kid, but now it was just something else in my way. I kicked at it angrily as I scuffed along, going nowhere, anywhere, just going.

I found myself in Central Park. All around me kids were playing—laughing, shouting, having snowball fights, sliding down hills on hunks of cardboard. A snowball bounced off my back and I heard Mickey's voice shouting for me to join in, but I just kept going.

The voices faded away and I kept on walking, deeper into the park than I've been in years. After a while, up ahead, a bunch of gray shapes loomed dimly through the snow. It looked like some kind of a junkyard, but why would there be a junkyard in Central Park? As I got closer I realized that it must be that Hooverville I'd heard about. I stopped a moment, remembering Mama's warnings, but then curiosity drew me on.

I walked slowly, trying not to stare at the jungle of makeshift shacks. Some of them were made from wooden packing crates, some just from cardboard. There were a few old army tents, a broken-down milk wagon, some rusted-out cars—just about anything a person could crawl inside of. There were folks scattered around inside and out, mostly men, but a woman here and there. I didn't see any kids. A group of people were huddled around an old metal barrel in which a fire burned. They wore filthy coats and had rags wrapped around their heads and hands. Some had rags on their feet, too. A few of them looked at me curiously as I walked by. Others gave me angry glances. Most didn't look at all, or if they did they just stared with those empty, unseeing eyes that Ma talks about.

I couldn't help wondering as I walked, was Pa standing around a barrel like that somewhere, dirty and ragged? As I reached the outer edge of the settlement I saw something that slowed my steps. Sitting inside an old piano crate was a woman who looked strangely familiar. I stood still for a moment, trying to figure out where I'd seen her before. Then I remembered—Luther White's ma! But no, it couldn't be. Luther's ma was always so neat and proper. This woman was filthy, sprawled on an old mattress, wrapped up in a dirty blanket, her hair stringy with grease. Still, the resemblance was striking.

"Mrs. White?" I ventured.

The woman stared straight ahead, seeming not to hear.

"Mrs. White?" I repeated, louder this time. The head lolled in my direction and a pair of blank eyes met mine briefly, then turned away again.

There was a sudden crashing in the bushes beside me, and I turned just as someone burst out of the woods and ran directly into me. I staggered back a few steps, but kept my balance. The stranger had dropped some bundles in the collision and fell to his knees to pick them up. I stooped to help him, then jerked back. The "bundles" were dead pigeons, their heads dangling limply from their twisted necks.

"Jesus," I whispered, "What the . . ."

My voice caught in my throat. The face that looked up into mine was Luther White's.

"Luther?" I said.

Luther quickly shoved the pigeons inside his coat and stood up.

"Get lost," he said.

"But Luther, it's me, Danny."

Luther went over and dumped the pigeons inside the piano crate, then he came back and grabbed the front of my jacket.

"I said get lost," he repeated.

I stared at him. "Luther, I just want to help."

The hold on my jacket tightened.

"My name ain't Luther," he said, "and I ain't never seen you before, and if you ain't outta here in five seconds, ain't nobody ever gonna see you again. Got it?"

"Yeah." I nodded. "I got it."

He let me go, and I stood staring a moment longer into his proud, angry eyes.

"I'm sorry," I said. "I must have been mistaken."

THIRTY-TWO

❧

The snow had gotten deeper and it took me a long time to get home. The streetlamps were on by the time I reached our block, and a huge mound of snow, piled high by the plow, stood in front of our stoop. The whole neighborhood was out, playing king of the mountain.

"Hey, Dan," shouted Mickey, "where've you been? Come on up."

"Nah. I got homework."

"Come on," called Maggie, "there won't be any school tomorrow."

A snowball grazed my head, then another hit me square in the mouth. Suddenly king of the mountain sounded like a great idea. I fought my way up the hill, flinging aside everybody in my path. Mickey was at the top. I came up behind him, shoved both my knees into the backs of his, making them buckle, gave him a sideways push, and down he went.

"King of the mountain," I shouted, beating my chest.

Maggie tackled me around the knees, knocking me off balance, but I grabbed her around the waist as I went down, pulling her with me. We tumbled head over heels until we landed at the bottom, her on her back on the ground, and me on top of her. I grabbed her wrists and pinned them down.

"Say uncle," I said.

Maggie bit her lip and struggled to get free. Maggie would rather die than say uncle. I laughed, secretly liking the feel of her body against mine.

"Say uncle," I yelled again.

A great force suddenly shoved me sideways and a heavy foot came down on my head, grinding my face into the snow. I came up sputtering to see Harry Sullivan scrambling right over me and up the snow mound. I lunged for his leg and missed. Harry let out a whooping laugh and kept going.

"King of the mountain," he shouted when he got to the top.

I scrambled up after him.

"Come on!" he shouted. "Come up and get your face shoved in the snow again."

He kicked out at my face as I neared the top. He wasn't fooling around. The kick probably would've broken my jaw if it'd landed square. As it was I ended up with a stinging blow to the ear. I rolled over and grabbed the foot he'd kicked with, and I twisted.

Harry's heavy body crashed over mine and we rolled together down the hill, him landing on top.

"Now *you* say uncle," he growled, pinning me the same way I'd pinned Maggie.

I struggled against his weight and he brought his knee up and ground it down painfully between my legs.

"Say uncle," he repeated, huffing with exertion. "Or are you gonna call your daddy? Oh, that's right. Your daddy run off, didn't he? I forgot your daddy run off. . . ."

All the anger that had been building inside me for weeks suddenly boiled up and blew. I was punching, biting, kicking, thrashing. The next thing I knew, I was on top and Harry was on the bottom. My hands closed around his neck.

"My pa didn't run off!" I shouted. "You take that back."

Harry gasped and tried to push me off, but my arms were like steel. I could have killed him if I wanted to, and he knew it.

"F-Frank," he gasped. "F-Frank, h-h-help!"

I looked up sharply, ready to take on Frank, too, if I had to. But Frank made no move to help his brother. He was actually smiling, seeming to enjoy the whole thing. Something about that drained all the fire out of me. Harry's own brother hated him.

I let Harry go, and he lay there for a while, rubbing his neck and gasping for breath. Then slowly he got to his feet. I actually felt sorry for him.

"Hey, Harry," I said.

He scowled at me. "What?"

"What do you say we forget all this and start over?" I reached out my hand to shake. Harry looked at my hand, then he looked at the crowd of faces that had gathered around us. Then he spit in my hand and walked away.

I shook my head and wiped my hand off in the snow. Frank still stood beside me. He and I stared at each other a moment, then he stuck his hand out. I took it and smiled. He smiled back, then he looked up the street after Harry and his smile faded.

"I guess I better go," he said.

"You don't have to," I told him.

Frank looked around the circle of faces, then he looked at Harry again.

"I guess I do," he said. "He's my brother."

I nodded. "Well, come around anytime," I told him.

"Thanks," he said, "maybe I will . . . sometime," then he shoved his hands in his pockets and followed Harry up the street.

"C'mon," said Mickey, starting up the mountain again.

"Nah," I said, "I'm tired." I sat down on the stoop and watched for a while. I found myself thinking about Luther White and his mother. What had happened to change them so in the past few months? Where was the rest of Luther's family? Where was his pa? Had he run off?

Then it wasn't Luther's pa I was wondering about. It was my own. Could Pa have run off like Harry said? The Pa I knew wouldn't—but suppose he'd changed, like Luther, or worse, like Luther's ma. How would we ever know? How long could Ma and I go on waiting?

I climbed the stairs with all those questions still spinning around in my head, but when I pushed the door open and saw Ma bent over her writing paper, I knew the answer to the last one at least. We'll go on waiting forever.

THIRTY-THREE

Friday, February 17, 1933

I'm not sure when I started thinking about going after
Pa, but now that I've started, I can't stop. It's become the most important thing in my life. I'm not
sure when I'll go. I'll have to wait until after the baby's born at least, maybe 'til school gets out. I've been
listening to "True Detective Mystery" on the radio,
trying to study up as much as I can on following clues
and tracking people down. I already know my first
clue—New London, Connecticut—the place Pa's
letter came from. It ought to be easy enough to find
someone there who'll recognize Pa's picture and who
knows where he's gone. I've begun to spend all my
spare time dreaming about how I will find him, about
what he'll say when he first lays eyes on me, about
how Mama will look when I bring him home again.

Just making my plans, knowing that I will go,

helps to lift the weight from my chest. I wish I could let Mama in on my plans and lighten her burden, too, but I can't. She would never agree to let me go.

Mama's headaches and the swelling in her legs have begun again, just like with Maureen.

A couple of weeks ago when she was ironing, she suddenly put the iron down and staggered over to a chair, holding her head.

"I'm going to call Doc Davis," I told her.

"No, no," she said. "It's just a spell. It'll pass."

"It's not a spell, Mama. It's the same as it was before," I argued. "Look at your legs. They're as fat as old Mrs. Tharp's downstairs."

That made her smile. "Well, thank you kindly for the compliment," she said, "but I'm all right. I'll call the doctor if I need him."

"No you won't. You're too proud because you know we can't pay."

"Pride's a fine thing, but I'm not fool enough to die of it, Danny."

I believed her and I felt better for it. But I guess *I* was the fool, because today I came home to find Doc Davis's hat on the table, the curtain pulled over Ma's door, and Mrs. Riley washing out bloody towels in the sink.

"Now don't go jumping to conclusions," Mrs. Riley warned when she caught sight of my face. "It's not as bad as it looks. Just a little spotting is all. You run along back outside and I'll call you when the doctor is through."

"No," I said, heading for the bedroom door. Mrs. Riley scurried over and parked herself in my path.

"You'll embarrass your mother to death if you go in there now," she said. "Run along, like I said."

"No," I repeated.

Mrs. Riley put her hands on her hips and shook her head. "You are as stubborn as a mule," she said. "All right then, stay, but you sit in that chair over there and wait until the doctor comes out."

I picked Maureen up from the floor where she was playing with her coffeepot and did as Mrs. Riley said. I could hear the murmur of voices on the other side of the curtain, and I strained to listen, but Mrs. Riley was carrying on a nonstop, one-sided conversation that seemed designed to frustrate me.

The voices on the other side of the curtain began to rise, and Mrs. Riley's rose with them.

"Mrs. Riley, you're shouting," I told her.

"Am I?" She laughed nervously. "You know, I think it comes of having nine children. The girls are always telling me, 'Mama, you're shouting,' and I don't even realize it. Sometimes I think . . ."

She went on and on, but I paid no attention. Mama and Doc Davis were shouting now, too, and I could hear them clearly over Mrs. Riley's prattle.

"I can't," Mama shouted.

"You don't, and I won't be responsible for the baby's life, or your own."

"But what of my ironing?"

"You should have thought of that six months

ago. I told you another child would be the death of you."

A shiver of fear ran up my spine, and I hugged Maureen tighter.

"I'm a Catholic, doctor," came Mama's reply.

"You're a fool, woman!" the doctor shouted. "Don't you realize you've two other children to care for?"

A silence followed, and I looked over at Mrs. Riley. She made a face and shook her head. "Don't go paying him no mind," she said. "Doc just loves to scare people."

When Doc spoke again, it was obvious that his temper had cooled some. "Now, I'll see you through this," he said, "and the baby, too, but you damn well better be in that bed every time I check on you. And you send that boy of yours at the first sign of any more bleeding. Understand?"

Mama mumbled something, and a moment later the curtain was jerked aside and Doc strode out. He nodded shortly to Mrs. Riley and me, picked up his hat, and left without a word.

Mrs. Riley shook her head. "Some bedside manner," she said. "If he wasn't such a good doctor I'd have sent him packing years ago." She took Maureen from my arms and nodded toward the bedroom doorway.

Mama was lying on her back, staring at the ceiling. When she saw me her eyes grew moist.

"Oh, Danny," she said, "what're we gonna do now?"

I remembered what she had said that time, about it giving her comfort to write to Pa, even though she didn't know where to send the letters. I went over to her dresser and took out her letter paper.

"Here," I told her. "You're gonna write to Pa, and I'm gonna start the laundry."

THIRTY-FOUR

Saturday, March 11, 1933

Ma always made it look so easy. She never told me the laundry had a mind of its own. By the end of the first week I had a permanent backache; my hands were red raw; I couldn't get the smell of Octagon soap and bleach out of my nose; and I had burns on my hands, my arms, and even my chin—I'm not going to even try and explain how I managed that.

Take everything I just said and double it, and that'd just about cover the second week. Meals were makeshift at best, and we probably wouldn't have survived without donations from ladies in the building. By last Saturday, despite Mama's constant praise and encouragement, I was feeling pretty low. The only thing that saved me was that it was Inauguration Day, and somehow I believed that President Roosevelt was going to make things better. Mama and I sat by the radio and listened to his speech.

"I am certain," he said, "that my fellow Americans expect that on my induction into the Presidency I will address them with a candor and a decision which the present situation of our nation impels." He said some other big words, then he said something that gave me hope. "This great nation will endure as it has endured, will revive and will prosper. So, first of all, let me assert my firm belief that the only thing we have to fear is fear itself. . . ."

As he went on talking, I began to believe that he was right. America can lick the depression, and if America can lick the depression, I can sure lick the laundry. I went at it again, more determined than ever, and by the end of this week, I got it down to a science. Laundry into the tub to soak at night. Get up at half past four. Scrub, soap, and bleach. Rinse. Laundry back into the tub with bluing. Go shine shoes. Come home. Rinse again, twist, and hang out. Go to school. Come home. Take the wash in, dampen, and roll up. Do homework. Fix supper. Iron and listen to the radio. Give Maureen her bath and put her to bed. Put in another load to soak for the morning. Iron again until bedtime. There's no time for anything else. I haven't seen Mickey in weeks, or any of the other guys, either, except in school.

I'm managing, though, and I felt pretty good about myself this morning as I loaded the last of the laundry into the wagon and headed down to Miss Emily's.

Sadie, unlike her usual jolly self, seemed anxious and fretful when she let me in.

"Something wrong, Sadie?" I asked.

"Oh, no. Nothin', child. Nothin' for you to worry your head about." She fidgeted absentmindedly about the kitchen with her washrag, too distracted to remember to tell Miss Emily that I'd come.

"Come on, Sadie," I insisted. "I can see that something's wrong."

"Oh, it's the bank," she blurted out, her eyes near tears. "The bank's gone and closed its doors, just like that, without a word of warning."

"Don't worry, Sadie," I told her, feeling very smart because we'd just discussed the banking crisis in school. "That's only because of the bank holiday. President Roosevelt closed the banks to keep everybody from panicking and taking their money out. I'm sure your bank will open up again. Lots of them already have."

Sadie shook her head. "I shore wish I could believe that," she said, "but that bank holiday ended on Thursday, and my bank is still locked up tight."

It's true that lots of banks have gone out of business since the depression started, and lots of folks have lost their savings. There's a good chance that Sadie's bank will open up again, but I can't blame her for being scared. "Do you have a lot of money in it?" I asked.

Sadie twisted the washrag in her hands.

"Every week," she said, her voice hushed, "for ten years now, I been puttin' a little somethin' aside. Didn't tell a soul, not even my husband. My boy Jim, see, he's real smart and I said to myself, 'Sadie, that boy's gonna make somethin' of hisself. That boy is college material, and you just better be ready when the time comes around.' "

The tears spilled out of her eyes now and she dabbed at them with the rag. "Well, here it is, nearly time, and the bank's gone and closed up. Who would believe such a thing?" She heaved a sigh and her great bosom rose and fell with the weight of it.

I searched for something to say, something strong and comforting, then I remembered President Roosevelt's speech. I reached out and put my hand on her arm. "Sadie," I said solemnly, "you have nothing to fear but fear itself."

Sadie looked at me a moment, then her face cracked into a wide smile and a hearty laugh bubbled up from deep inside her. She threw her head back and laughed and laughed, her bosom shaking mightily, until tears rolled down her cheeks. I stared at her in complete confusion.

"Oh Lawd, Lawd," she said, slowing down at last and catching her breath. "Lawd, that felt good. Thank you, child. Ain't nothin' like a good laugh to put your problems back in perspective."

I shrugged, glad I'd helped, but not quite sure how I'd done it.

"Just a minute now," Sadie went on, "I'll go tell Miss Emily you're here."

I started unloading the wagon, and a few minutes later Sadie came back through the door, looking strangely white for a black person. She put the money into my hand, then she stood there, continuing to hold my hand in hers. Something in her look frightened me.

"Sadie? What is it?"

Sadie squeezed my hand and looked at me mournfully. "Miss Emily says," she began, "Miss Emily says the quality of your mama's work done fallen off some. She says she has found another laundress."

My mouth fell open and I could actually feel the blood draining from my face. I shook my head.

"No, Sadie . . . she can't mean that."

Sadie nodded her head sadly. "She mean it okay, child. Miss Emily don't say nothin' she don't mean."

I grabbed Sadie's arm desperately. "No, Sadie. She can't. She doesn't understand. It's my fault. Ma's pregnant and sick. I been doin' the laundry. I admit, I didn't do so good the first couple of weeks, but I got it down now. I'm doin' good now—look."

I grabbed a tablecloth from the pile and handed it to her. "See? Take this. Show it to her, please. She's got to give me another chance."

Sadie took the tablecloth and nodded.

"All right, child, all right," she said. "Calm yourself. Remember what you told me just now, 'bout fear. I'll see what I can do."

Sadie disappeared through the door again, and I dropped to my knees and crossed myself. "Please, God," I whispered, "make her give me another chance."

It was quiet awhile, then I heard Sadie's voice rising in anger. "But I just told you 'bout his mama.

He's tryin' so hard. Look at this cloth here. Why it's just as pretty as you please."

"It has a scorch on it."

"Just a little, bitty scorch. You can hardly see it. Think of his mama, Miss Emily. She done give you a lot of good years."

"For which she was adequately paid. I owe her nothing. Times like they are, these people ought to know better than to keep breeding like a bunch of sows. It's just plain ignorant."

A few seconds later Sadie burst through the door and yanked me to my feet. "Get up off your knees, child. It's blasphemy in this house." She whisked off her apron and hung it on a hook by the door, then she grabbed her coat off another hook and started to put it on.

"You and me is walkin' out of here," she said, breathing hard and fast, "and ain't neither one of us ever comin' back."

I was scared, and I was mad, but I still had enough of my wits about me to know I couldn't let Sadie do what she was about to do. I grabbed ahold of her coat sleeve and pulled her back.

"No, Sadie," I told her, "you can't do this."

"Just you watch me," she said, pulling her arm free.

I grabbed on again. "Sadie, listen. What about your boy Jim? What about your other kids? Jobs are hard to come by, real hard. You know that. You told me yourself that your husband's out of work. You can't do this. Think of your family."

Sadie didn't pull away this time. She stood still and her shoulders sagged, and all the fight seemed to seep out of her, like air out of a balloon. She pulled her coat off slowly and hung it up, then she grabbed me and hugged me against her great chest.

"You remember one thing, child," she said quietly. "This is just a short path we walkin'. The long road, the good road, lies ahead. And when we get there, you can count on one thing. Folks like Miss Emily that has spent this life lookin' down is sure 'nough gonna spend all eternity lookin' up."

THIRTY-FIVE

Friday, March 31, 1933

Mama said we shouldn't let on to the neighbors about losing the laundry business. She said they'd only try to pitch in and help, and none of them have anything to spare. She said we'd manage somehow.

I went door to door and shop to shop, looking for any kind of work I could find and turning up nothing, day after day. Every spare minute I had I spent down on the street with my shoeshine box, but there seemed to be more shoeshine boys than ever, and less business to go around. At mealtimes I began to know how Pa must've felt. Here I was, eating a portion that could have gone to Ma or Maureen. Me, fit and able-bodied, taking food from the sick and the small.

I hit on the idea of telling Ma I'd found a job at a restaurant that would give me my noonday dinner in exchange for washing dishes. She said it seemed slave wages to her, but I insisted that I wanted to do it and she gave me permission. So I just stopped coming home from school at noontime, and at supper I pretended like I was still full from stuffing myself at the restaurant and pushed most of my portion off on Ma and Maureen.

That worked fine for about two weeks, but today as I was climbing the stairs after school, everything suddenly swirled around and went black. Next thing I knew I was lying in a heap at the bottom of the stairs with a sore head and an aching back and a gang of Rileys bending over me.

"What're you all staring at?" I growled.

"You," said Maggie.

"Why?"

"Because you just passed out and rolled down the stairs, knocking half of us over on the way, and we thought it was a little odd."

I scowled at her and started to sit up, but suddenly everybody disappeared in a painful swirl of colored lights, and I slumped back down again.

"Danny?"

It was Maggie's voice coming through the swirl.

"Danny, should we get help?"

"No," I groaned. "Just leave me alone."

I heard Maggie send her brother and sisters on up the stairs, then I felt her arm sliding under my head.

"Come on," she said, "sit up slowly . . . and don't try to do it all yourself. Let me help."

I didn't have a lot of energy and it was easier to

give in than to argue, so I let her help me to a sitting position. My head swam again and I felt myself starting to sway.

"Put your head down between your knees a minute," Maggie directed.

I closed my eyes and did as she said. The whirling slowed down until at last I opened my eyes and the hallway stayed in one place.

Maggie sat beside me, her eyes studying mine.

"You're starving," she said.

"Don't be stupid," I told her, "I'm just . . ."

"I'm not stupid and you know it. I can see there haven't been any linens on the line in weeks. Your Ma and Maureen seem to be doing okay, but you're starving. Why?"

I should've known better than to try and fool Maggie. Maggie is as street smart as they come. I figured I might as well let her in on my dishwashing scheme. She listened and nodded, and I even think she was a little bit impressed.

"Nice try," she said, "except for one thing."

"What's that?"

"You keep on getting weaker like this and you won't even be able to handle your shoeshine business. Then where will you be?"

I shrugged. "I don't know," I said, "but I know I can't eat at home. There just isn't enough to go around."

Maggie nodded. "You don't have to."

"What do you mean?"

"Can you stand yet?"

"I think so."

Maggie helped me to my feet and I stood still for a moment, letting my head settle.

"Can you walk?"

"Yeah, I'm okay."

"Let's go then."

"Where to?"

"Supper."

"Supper?"

"Just follow me."

Maggie led the way down the street and around to the back door of the bakery. She knocked and a burly man in an apron opened the door. His hairy arms were white with flour. The wonderful smell of fresh, hot bread drifted out and started my mouth watering.

"Hello there, Maggie," the man said pleasantly enough. "How you doin'?"

"Fine thanks, Mr. Lizauskas. Any crusts today?"

"As a matter of fact, there's a couple of nice, thick ones I been saving just for you." He brought out a small sack and handed it to her.

"Thanks, Mr. Lizauskas."

"You're welcome, Maggie."

The door closed and Maggie opened the bag and looked in. "Mmm," she said, "pumpernickel."

I stared at her. "Maggie," I said, "this is begging."

A look of pretended shock appeared on her face. "No! Really?"

"Come on, Maggie. This isn't right."

Maggie shook her head and frowned. "Okay mister," she said. "You sit there on your high horse if you want to, but I'm warning you, you're gonna get awfully hungry up there." She crumpled the bag shut and walked away.

The idea of that fresh bread getting away was too much to bear in my present condition.

"Maggie, wait." I hurried to catch up. "Look, you're right. I'm sorry. Beggars can't be choosers, I guess. Huh?"

She ignored me until we got to Sarge's hot dog stand on the corner. She pulled out the two crusts of pumpernickel and plastered them both with mustard. I waited for Sarge to swat her, but he didn't seem to mind.

"Thanks, Sarge," she said when she was done, giving Sarge a salute.

"Welcome, Miss Maggie," said Sarge, saluting in return.

She turned and held one of the crusts out to me.

"Just hold it," she said. "Don't eat it yet."

I looked at it and swallowed down the flood of water that filled my mouth, not daring to argue again. Next stop was the deli, where we got an end of cheese and one of salami. Maggie took the cheese and gave the salami to me.

"Salami gives me bad breath," she said. "Now eat. Whatever else we get, we take home."

We sat down in an alley and rested while we ate. Charity or not, that food sure tasted good.

"Are they always this nice?" I asked her, meaning the shopkeepers.

She laughed. "Nah, some of them would just as soon spit on you as look at you, but we stay away from them. For the most part, though, folks are pretty willing to share whatever extra they got."

"That's really nice," I said.

"Yeah." Maggie nodded. "How you feeling? Any better?"

"Lots, thanks."

"Good. Let's get going."

Next stop was a vegetable cart where we got a couple of tomatoes that had fallen on the ground and split and some potatoes with bad spots. At a fruit stand we picked up some brown bananas, and another vegetable man gave us some onions that were starting to sprout. The pork store had some bones to spare, and the meat market some chicken necks. We ended up behind St. Cecilia's Convent, where a small crowd of kids waited to divvy up whatever the nuns had left over after dinner. To my surprise, Kitty was there. She seemed embarrassed to see me. So did most of the other kids.

"It's all right," Maggie told them all. "This is Danny. I'll vouch for him."

Her word seemed enough to put them at ease.

"We each take a different route," Maggie told me. "We get more that way. Then we meet here and share whatever we get. I'll show you some of the other routes, then you'll be on your own."

"On my own?"

"Yes. I told you, you get more that way."

It finally dawned on me what she was talking about. "You mean, you . . . you expect *me* to beg?" I stammered.

Maggie recoiled as if I'd slapped her. Fury burned in her eyes. She had given me a bag of food, now she snatched it away without a word and stormed out of the alley.

Kitty came up beside me, her face deep-red with shame. "Don't you tell Mickey about this," she whispered hoarsely, then turned and fled after her sister.

I looked at the small group of kids that still waited behind the church. Some of them glared at me. Others wouldn't look up. They didn't welcome strangers, I realized. They came together secretly, out of need, and each new person in the group meant that much less to go around. They had been willing to take me in on Maggie's say-so, and now I'd made a fool of her. Worse, I'd belittled her. I'd belittled them all.

I backed away from their accusing stares and hurried out into the street. Maggie and Kitty were up by the tunnel already. I ran to catch up.

"Maggie, wait," I yelled.

She put her head down and walked faster. I caught up with her in the tunnel and grabbed her arm. She pulled away, and she and Kitty started to run. I caught her again, and Kitty kept going and disappeared around the end of the tunnel.

Maggie tried to pull away. "Let me go," she shouted, pounding at me with her free hand.

Suddenly my head began to swim again. All the running had been too much. I felt myself falling backwards, then my head hit the tunnel wall and I slid to the ground. The last sounds I heard were Maggie's running footsteps echoing in the distance.

"Danny? Danny, are you all right?"

I opened my eyes and Maggie's face swam dizzily in front of me.

"I thought you ran away," I mumbled.

"I did," she said. "And if I was smart I'd have kept on going."

"But you didn't."

"No. Don't ask me why. Are you okay or not?"

I reached back and felt the lump on my head. It wasn't bleeding. "Yeah, I guess so."

"Good. Good-bye."

Maggie started to stomp off again.

"Maggie, wait." I jumped to my feet, then staggered back against the wall again. I put my aching head down in my hands, then I felt an arm around my shoulders, steadying me.

"You are the biggest pain in the neck that ever lived," I heard Maggie grumble. "Come on. I'll help you home."

I leaned against her and we started to make our way slowly out of the tunnel. When we got to our stoop I sat down to rest on the top step.

"I guess you can make it from here," Maggie said, and turned away.

I grabbed her hand. "Maggie, wait."

She frowned, but she didn't pull away this time.

"I'm really sorry about what I said back there. It came out sounding like I think I'm better than you, and I don't, honest. You're better than I'll ever be. I'm just not used to this stuff, Maggie. Pa always had so much pride. . . ."

Maggie snorted. "Do you know what pride is?" she snapped. "Pride is a word rich people invented to ease their consciences about poor people. 'Oh, we can't help *them*. It would hurt their *pride*.' I can't afford to be proud, Danny. I'm not rich enough."

"I don't believe that," I told her.

She looked away.

"Anyway, thanks," I said.

"For what?"

"For showing me the ropes. I'll get used to it."

"No, you won't," Maggie said quietly. "You'll do it because you have to, but you'll never get used to it."

THIRTY-SIX

Ma was sitting at the kitchen table when I got home, wearing the better of her two maternity dresses. She looked paler than usual.

"What are you doing out of bed?" I demanded.

She looked at me. Her face was so weary.

"I been out," she said.

"Out where?"

"The City Relief Bureau."

The words hit me like a hard punch in the stomach.

"Relief?" I gasped. "We're on welfare?"

Mama looked away and said nothing.

"Why?" I asked her.

She looked back at me. "I'm not blind, Danny. You're wastin' away. There's no restaurant, is there?"

It was my turn to say nothing.

Mama sighed and shook her head. "I shoulda known," she said.

She looked so heartbroken and defeated that I went over and dropped to my knees beside her. "It's all right, Mama," I said, squeezing her arm. "We won't be on welfare long. It's just to get us through. Look." I picked up the bag Maggie had given me. "I been begging, too."

"Oh, Daniel, you haven't!"

"Yes, I have. See for yourself."

She opened the bag and looked inside.

"Mother o' God, what's become of us," she whispered. She looked at me like she didn't know whether to laugh or cry, then I smiled and we both burst out laughing.

"Aren't we awful?" said Mama.

"Terrible," I agreed, and we laughed some more. Suddenly Mama's laughter gave way to tears and she covered her face with her hands.

"Mama?"

"I'm sorry," she whispered, "it's just . . . the thought of you, out begging . . . and, oh, Daniel, that place. The way people looked at me, the questions they asked. . . . And all for this."

She opened her purse and dumped it out on the table. Six dollars fell out, and some change.

"That's it?" I asked.

She nodded. "Six dollars and sixty cents a week. That'll hardly feed us, Daniel, let alone pay the rent. We're still not gonna make it."

I got up and put my arm around her shoulders. "Sure we will," I told her. "Somehow we will."

She sat there shaking her head for a long time, then suddenly she straightened and her eyes flew open.

"Why, of course," she said. "Why didn't I think of it before? We'll sell the front-room furniture."

"The front-room furniture!" I stared at her. The front-room furniture was Mama's pride and joy. She and Pa had scrimped and saved for years to buy it. I can still remember the day it was delivered, the way Mama spread out her skirt and plopped herself right in the middle of the sofa.

"How do I look?" she'd said, as excited as a little kid. "How do I look?"

"Just like the queen herself, darlin'," Pa had told her. "Just like the queen herself. . . ."

"No, Ma," I said, "don't sell the furniture."

"My mind is made up," Mama insisted. "You'll be puttin' a sign down in the hall tomorrow."

"But Ma, you don't understand. The way things are you'll be lucky to get a tenth what it's worth. You might as well give it away."

"A tenth is better than nothing," said Mama, and she snapped her mouth shut in a way that said "conversation closed."

Just then the door buzzer sounded.

"Go see who that is, will you, Daniel?" said Mama. "And then go over and get Maureen from the Rileys'."

"Okay, Ma." I went into the front room, my heart

sinking at the sight of the furniture, and stuck my head out the window. Mr. Twiddle was smiling up at me.

"Collecting!" he sang out cheerfully.

I fought back a terrible urge to spit in his face. "Just a minute," I grumbled.

I went back to Mama in the kitchen. "It's Twiddle," I said, wrinkling up my nose.

Mama rolled her eyes toward the ceiling.

"Don't pay him, Mama," I insisted. "Just think what that quarter would buy."

Mama stared at the two quarters that lay on the kitchen table, then slowly she shook her head. She picked one up and put it in my hand.

"No," she said tiredly. "We've got to pay him. Pa said whatever happened not to . . . let the . . . insurance . . . lapse."

She spoke these last words slowly, as if something were dawning on her. When her eyes looked up at mine, I saw an awful fear there.

"Mama, what is it?"

Her face had gone white as a sheet, and her breath was coming in gasps.

"Mama, are you all right?"

"Yes . . . yes." She clutched her chest and looked away.

"Are you sure, Mama? Is it the baby? Are you sick?"

"No, no, nothing like that. Just . . . Go pay Mr. Twiddle, Danny. I'll be okay."

When I got back Mama was breathing normally again, but she still seemed unusually pale.

"Help me to bed, will ya, Danny?" she said. "I'm feelin' a bit weak."

"Should I call the doctor?" I asked when I'd gotten her safely into bed.

"No," she whispered wearily, "just leave me alone a bit. Okay, love?" She pulled the sheet up over her face and turned away.

I went out to the kitchen and threw the chicken necks in a pot, hating Mr. Twiddle for upsetting Mama so.

THIRTY-SEVEN

〜

I woke up in the middle of the night with my bladder bursting, cursing myself for being such a pig and drinking three bowls of chicken soup before bed. I sure didn't want to get out of my warm bed and go to that cold, dark, creepy toilet. I lay still awhile, trying to convince my body that it could wait 'til morning, but my body was in no mood to listen. It got to be a matter of getting up or wetting the bed. Since I'm a little old for wetting the bed, I dragged myself out from under the covers.

So as not to wake Ma or Maureen I stumbled through the spare room and into the front room. Fuzzy-headed, I groped in the dark for the door, found the knob, and turned. Like a dam bursting, the door flew in at me, and a huge, dark figure lurched into the room.

"Huuhhh!" The air made a rushing sound as I

sucked it in. The man towered over me, his eyes rolling madly, his rancid breath coming out in great gasps. I stood there, frozen in fear, unable to run, unable to scream. He lunged a step closer.

"Aaaaghh!" At last a terrible scream burst from my lungs. A big hand closed over my mouth and nose. Another grabbed me and pinned me against the hulking body. I struggled to break free, but I was powerless in his grip.

Suddenly the room flooded with light and Mama stood in the spare room doorway, a carving knife in her hand. At the same instant a wave of Rileys surged through the front-room door. The man released me and stepped back.

"I didn't mean no harm. I didn't mean no harm," he blurted, lifting his hands in surrender.

Mama took a step forward. The knife trembled in her hand, but her face showed her determination to use it if need be.

"I didn't mean to hurt him," the man went on, his breathing loud and raspy. "Honest. I wouldn't hurt a fly. He just scared me so, screamin' like that."

"Who are you?" Mama demanded, holding the knife up over her swollen belly.

"Powers," said the man. "Hank Powers."

In the light he didn't seem so menacing. He was real tall, probably about six foot five, and homely— kind of like Abraham Lincoln, only with stringy yellow hair. He was skinny and flushed, and there were dark circles under his eyes.

"Powers?" Mrs. Riley repeated, cocking her head to one side and giving him the once over.

"That's right, ma'am," the man said. He licked his lips. They were swollen and cracked. Beads of sweat stood out on his forehead. "You must know my brother, Bert. He lives in this building. I was on my way up to his apartment when I stopped to rest on the landin' out there a minute. I guess I was leanin' against the door when the boy here pulled it open."

Mama and Mrs. Riley exchanged glances. Now that he mentioned it, this guy did sort of look like the Mr. Powers who used to live on the fourth floor.

Mama lowered the knife.

"Bert Powers and his family moved out a couple of months ago," she said.

Her words hit the man hard. His eyes rolled back wildly again, and his big body swayed.

"M-moved out," he stammered. "Wh-what d'ya mean, moved out?"

"Evicted," said Mrs. Riley gently. "Couldn't pay the rent."

The man's shoulders sagged. His head fell forward and lolled from side to side, like he couldn't hold it up no more.

"Mister?" asked Mama. "You okay?"

The man didn't answer. He just stood there, his head lolling like it was about to fall off his neck.

Mrs. Riley went over and touched his shoulder. "Mister?"

At her touch the man staggered forward a step, then crashed down heavily on one knee. The knee buckled and he fell over on his side and lay still. Mrs. Riley dropped to her knees beside him. She felt his head.

"Good Lord," she said, "he's burnin' up. Maggie, Kitty, help me get him up on the couch here. Danny, get dressed and run for Doc Davis."

I looked at her, then at Ma.

"Mama," I said, "we're not gonna keep him here?"

Mama hesitated, then she walked over, laid her knife on the table, and bent to look at the man.

"Do as Mrs. Riley says, Danny," she told me.

"But Ma, we don't even know him."

She looked at me. "He's sick and in need," she said. "We'll do what we can."

"But Mama . . ."

She touched a finger to her lips to silence me.

"Maybe somewhere," she said, "someone is doin' as much for yer pa."

THIRTY-EIGHT

Thursday, April 6, 1933

Hank came around fast.

"Takes more than a touch of the flu to keep an Okie dirt farmer down," he said.

Doc said it was more like pneumonia, and near starved like Hank was, he was lucky to live through it. Pneumonia or not, though, inside of a week Hank was up and around and caring more for us than we were for him.

"What're you doing way out here?" I asked him this morning as we were washing the dishes. "Oklahoma's a long way from New York."

"Welp," said Hank. He always says "welp" instead of "well."

"Welp, I lost my farm, then I lost my wife, then I guess I lost my mind for a while. Then one morning I woke up facedown in the dirt and I said to myself, 'Hank, you can't sink any lower than this. Ain't nowhere to go from here but up.' So I picked myself up, and I brushed myself off, and I wrote to my brother, Bert, and I said, 'I'm on my way to the big city, brother. Don't know when I'll get there, but I'm on my way.' "

"So, how'd you get here?"

"Walked."

"From Oklahoma?"

"Yep. Oh, I hitched a ride here and there, jumped a train or two, but mostly I walked."

"How long'd it take you?"

Hank poured a little more hot water from the kettle into the dishpan. "Let's see now," he mused. "What's this, March?"

"Beginning of April," I corrected him.

Hank handed me a wet bowl and counted on his fingers. "December, January, February, March . . . 'bout four months, I reckon."

I dried the bowl and shook my head. "My pa's been gone over five months now," I told him.

Hank nodded. "It ain't easy out there on the road," he said. "Things come up you ain't expectin'."

"What's it like?" I asked.

Hank put the oatmeal pot into the dishpan and started to scrub. He shook his head. "Hard times," he said, "same as here. You go through town after town, nothin' but boarded-up stores, For Rent signs, factories empty and still. Come through one stretch in Pennsylvania, weren't a single person in the whole town had a job. Not one. Lot of folks on the road, lot of folks—men, women, whole families. Country folks headin' for the city. City folks headin' for the country. Everybody hopin' things'll be better somewheres else. Counted over one hundred men tryin' to jump the same freight train one night."

Hank scrubbed harder and harder as he talked, like he was trying to take his anger out on the pot. What he was saying didn't make me feel too hopeful about Pa. Maybe he noticed, because he suddenly changed his tune.

"Ain't all bad, though, I'll tell you. Folks is reachin' out to one another in ways I ain't never seen before. Saw a widow's farm go up for auction in Missouri. Her neighbors showed up by the hundreds with shovels and picks and axes, just darin' anyone to make a bid. One of 'em bought the farm for a dollar, and gave it back to the widow. Times like that, you get to feelin' we can lick this thing, if we hang together."

I nodded. It was a nice story, but I didn't see how it was gonna help Pa.

Hank dried his big hands on the dishrag and touched me gently on the shoulder. "There's a lot of good, carin' folks out there lendin' a hand, boy," he said. "Folks like your ma. Don't you give up hope now, you hear?"

I smiled. "I won't, Hank."

"Good. Now, why don't you go see if your ma is done with her oatmeal while this water's still warm."

Ma was sitting up in bed, just finishing her bowl.

"How is Mr. Powers this morning?" she asked.

"Seems fit as a fiddle to me."

Mama nodded, but the news didn't seem to make her happy.

"Something wrong, Mama?"

She lowered her voice.

"It's just that . . . we can't afford to be keepin' him any longer, Danny. We've little enough food, and we've got to be sellin' the furniture. The rent's overdue."

I nodded, feeling unexpectedly sad. It had been nice, even for a short time, to have a man in the house again.

"I'll tell him," I said.

When I came back out into the kitchen, Hank had his coat on and was tying his few belongings up in a handkerchief.

"Where are you going?" I asked, wondering if he'd overheard.

"Welp," he said, "I guess it's about time this old sodbuster was moving on."

"Where'll you go, Hank?"

He shrugged. "Nowhere in particular."

I nodded. "Do you suppose you could do me a favor?" I asked.

"Name it, my friend."

"If you happen to run into a big old Irish guy, name of Dan Garvey, would you send him on home?" My voice trembled a little and I looked away, embarrassed.

Hank tousled my hair.

"I shore will, son. I shore will."

229

THIRTY-NINE

Late in the afternoon, as I was finishing up my homework, a loud knock—or I should say, more like a loud kick—came at the door. I jumped up and pulled it open to see a pile of bulging grocery sacks balanced on top of a pair of long legs.

"Who is it?" called Mama from the bedroom.

A big, horsey smile appeared around one of the sacks.

"It's Hank," I shouted, not quite believing what I was seeing.

"Welp, you gonna ask me in," said Hank, "or you gonna make me sit out here and eat this stuff all by myself?"

I pulled the door wide, and Hank maneuvered over and dumped his bundles on the kitchen table.

"What'd you do?" I asked. "Rob a bank?"

"Nah." He laughed. "The banks ain't got no money."

"Then how . . ."

"I'll get to that. I'll get to that. You just start puttin' this stuff away. I gotta go get your ma."

Fortunately it was still chilly enough outside to use the window box, because we didn't have any ice. I slid the kitchen window open and started loading the food out there. Hank carried the old rocker into the kitchen and got Mama all settled with pillows and blankets, her feet propped up on a kitchen chair. Then he whipped Maureen up off the floor and sat down with her on his lap. He ignored Ma and me and pretended like he was talking just to her.

"You know, Mo-reen," he told her.

That's how Hank says her name, Mo-reen.

"You know, Mo-reen, all my life I been hearin' about this feller or that feller that had some kind of good fortune come to him 'cause he was in the right place at the right time, and I been saying to myself, 'Hank Powers? How come you always in the *wrong* place, at the *wrong* time?' "

Maureen stared up at him so funny I almost had to laugh. Her little mouth was open and her brow all wrinkled up, looking for all the world like she was really pondering everything he said.

"Yup," Hank went on, "that's what I always said. Then what do you know? Here I am, just walkin' down the street today, and all of a sudden, *SLAM! BAM!* There I am, in the right place, at the right time."

"Hank," I said, nearly splitting with curiosity by now, "are you gonna get to the point or not?"

At that point Hank stood up, dropped Maureen in my lap, and started dancing around the room like he was putting on a show.

"I was walking down the street, see," he said, strutting across the room like a long-legged chicken, "just the other side of them tracks out front, when what do I see rising up out of the ground, right in the middle of New York City, but a horse!"

I had to laugh. He made it sound like such a miracle.

"We got lots of horses, Hank," I told him. "That's the stable over there. It runs under the whole block."

"Welp, I know that now," said Hank, "but I didn't know it then. All I know is here comes this horse up from under the ground, and she's runnin' for all she's worth, and behind her she's draggin' some poor feller what's got his foot tangled up in her traces. Welp, if there's one thing I know, it's how to handle a horse, so I grabbed ahold of her bridle as she went by and hung on, hoppin' along beside her and talkin' real easy. And I'm a-hoppin' and a-talkin' and a-hoppin' and a-talkin', until finally she starts slowing down some. I go right on a-hoppin' and a-talkin' a little while longer 'til she just stops and stands there wheezin' and a-blowin' just as nice as you please.

"Next thing I know, up from behind comes these four fellers all shoutin' and hollerin' to beat the band. They bent down and started checkin' over the poor guy that's been draggin' along behind all this while.

" 'Welp,' says one, 'he's gonna live, but he sure ain't gonna work for a while.'

" '*Damn,*' says another. Oh, pardon me, Miz Garvey. 'Darn,' says another. 'Where're we gonna find another man that knows horses like old Jake here?' "

At that Hank stopped talking and just stood there, grinning at us.

"You?" I shouted. "You got the job?"

"None other," said Hank, clapping his hands together and taking a bow.

I jumped up and slapped him on the back. "Congratulations, Hank," I said. "That's great."

Mama smiled, but she didn't say anything.

"Something wrong, Miz Garvey?" Hank asked.

"Of course not," said Mama. "I'm very happy for you, Mr. Powers."

Hank looked at her skeptically. "You're thinkin' about that feller, Jake, aren't you?" he said.

Mama shrugged apologetically. "Aye," she said. "I guess I couldna' help it."

Hank sighed and nodded. "Seems like that's always the way, don't it? One feller's got to lose for another to win. Maybe I shouldn'ta took the job."

Mama shook her head and waved his words away. "Now don't ya be silly. The poor man probably owes his life to ya, and ya said yerself he's not fit to work. Besides, you've had yer time of losin', Mr. Powers. Ya deserve to win."

Hank smiled again. "Thank you, ma'am," he said. "I'm glad you feel that way, 'cause I got a bit of a business proposition for ya."

Mama bent her head to one side and gave him a questioning look. "Aye?"

"Now that I'm a workin' man," said Hank, "I'll be needin' a place to stay and, welp, that couch of yours is real comfy, and I just thought . . ."

Mama blushed and looked down at her hands. She shook her head. "I'm sorry, Mr. Powers," she said quietly, "it just wouldn't be seemly, my husband away and all."

Hank pushed his hair back roughly and shifted from one foot to the other.

"I didn't mean nothin' improper, ma'am," he went on. "I just thought we could help each other out some is all."

Mama looked up again and he continued.

"See, here I am with some money and no place to stay, and here you are with plenty of room and . . . And I could pay four, maybe five dollars a week. I wouldn't bother you none. There's bathing facilities down at the stables, and I could take my meals out, and . . . Welp, the truth is, ma'am, it's an awfully big city, and I don't know another soul in the whole danged place. I mean, I know I could bunk down in the stables, but it smells awful bad down there, and the flies . . ."

Mama's eyes seemed to be growing larger and larger as Hank's speech went on and on. Now her mouth fell open and she held up her hand for Hank to stop. To my amazement, she nodded.

"Four dollars a week will be just fine, Mr. Powers," she said.

My mouth fell open so hard my teeth almost came loose.

"Ma!"

"Hush, Danny."

"I will not hush. You can't do this. What will the neighbors say?"

Mama chuckled. "Oh, I expect they'll say plenty."

"Ma! Have you lost your senses?"

Mama's smile faded. She looked at me steady and determined. "Daniel," she said, "I have been prayin' every waking moment of every day for a miracle that would let us stay in this apartment. The way I'm thinkin', Mr. Powers is our angel of delivery."

Hank threw his head back and laughed.

Mama shot him a sharp look.

"I'm sorry, ma'am," he said. "I didn't mean to laugh. It's just that . . . I been called a lot of things in my life, but that is a first, ma'am. That shore is a first."

Mama smiled. "The Lord works in strange ways, Mr. Powers," she said.

"Oh, I don't deny that, ma'am," said Hank. He slapped his knee and reached a hand out to Mama. "Then we got a deal?"

Mama leaned forward and put her hand out, too. "That we do, Mr. Powers."

Hank squeezed her small hand in his big one.

"I shore do wish you'd call me Hank," he said.

Mama smiled and gently pulled her hand away again. " 'Mr. Powers' suits me just fine," she told him.

FORTY

Monday, April 24, 1933

Mama hasn't been herself in weeks. Sometimes she's so quiet and sulky she hardly seems to know I'm around. Other times she's snappin' at every move I make. Nothing seems to please her. Like the day beer and wine became legal again. I was reading to her from the newspaper all about how these six big Clydesdales pulled a wagon right up to the Empire State Building and handed former Governor Al Smith a case of beer, and right in the middle of the story Ma burst into tears. I thought she'd be happy. It's the first step toward ending Prohibition.

I try to get her to listen to President Roosevelt whenever he comes on the radio. He gives these talks he calls "fireside chats," and they really make *me* feel better. He talks about how we're all Americans, and how we've been through tough times before, and how we can lick this depression if we just pull together. Sometimes he cheers Ma up a little, but not for long.

It seems to me a lot of good things are happening. The banks are doing better and there's this new thing called the Civilian Conservation Corps that's going to put a lot of people back to work. They get room and board and a dollar a day! I might even join up when I get a little older. Last month the Bonus army marched on Washington again. This time the people were fed, housed and doctored, and invited to the White House to talk with the president. Mrs. Roosevelt even went out and visited their camp. She really seems to care about people. I was just telling Ma today how much everybody seems to like Mrs. Roosevelt. They say she's quite a lady. Ma just grumbled, "I guess I'd be quite a lady, too, if I was in her shoes."

It's not like Ma to talk that way.

I told Hank about it when he got home from work, but he only laughed.

"Women get like that near the end of their time," he said. "Just stay out of her way. She'll be herself again, once the baby's come."

"But, Hank," I told him, "that's more than a month away. How am I gonna stay out of her way that long?"

Hank laughed again. "Tell you what," he said. "I'll go pick up some groceries and we'll fix her a nice supper and tell her a tall tale or two, cheer her up some. If you don't mind my company, that is."

"That'd be great, Hank," I said. Mostly Hank

keeps to himself, but every now and then a sack of groceries appears on our doorstep and Mama asks him to stay to supper, and he ends up spinning tall tales for us all evening. Mama seems to really enjoy his company. She says he's a regular midwestern *seanachie*.

Hank came back with a big sack of vegetables and some ground meat, and we set about making a stew.

"Tell me about where you're from, Hank," I asked him as we peeled potatoes together.

"What about it?"

"Is the depression as bad there as it is here?"

"Worse."

"Worse? How could it be worse?"

"Welp, for one thing it started a lot sooner," Hank said. "Started right after the war. See, times were good for farmers during the war. The army and the Allies needed lots of food. Crops were bringing good prices, so farmers planted more and more. Then suddenly the war ended. Not that I was sorry to see it end. War's a messy business and the sooner you're quit of it, the better. But that year farm prices dropped by half. Being a thick-headed lot, us farmers figured if we were only getting half as much money for our crops, we'd plant twice as many and break even."

"That makes sense," I told him.

"Except for one thing," said Hank. "The more we planted, the more we had to sell, and since there weren't no more need for it, prices went down even worse. Things has got so bad that these days corn is selling for three dollars and thirty-three cents a ton. You know what a ton is?"

I shrugged. "Sort of."

"Two thousand pounds," said Hank. "Do you know what it takes to grow and harvest two thousand pounds of corn?"

I was about to say no, but Hank didn't wait for an answer.

"A wagonload of oats won't buy a four-dollar pair of shoes," he went on. "A man can't live on that kind of money. Folks are getting desperate. Heard tell of a farmer that had three thousand sheep to get to market. It was gonna cost him a dollar ten a head to ship 'em, and they were only gonna bring a dollar a head at the market. He couldn't afford to ship 'em, and he couldn't afford to feed 'em anymore, so he slit their throats and dumped 'em in a ditch."

"Yuck," I said, my stomach turning at the thought. "That's awful."

Hank nodded. "That ain't the worst of it, though," he said. He stopped peeling and stood staring at the cupboard, like he was seeing something reflected in the glass. "The worst of it has been the drought. It started in '30, and it ain't let up yet; the sun's just blazin' up there, cruel and white, day after day after day. First off the corn shriveled on the stalks. At night you could hear it rattlin' like dry paper in the wind. Next the ponds and the streams dried up, then the cows stopped giving milk. Lisbeth, my wife . . ."

Hank hesitated a moment and licked his lips, as if even the thought of the drought had dried them out. I'd never heard him mention his wife's name before, and when he spoke again there was a note of sadness in his voice.

"Lisbeth got skinny as a crow. We didn't have no young-uns. It was always a sorrow to us, 'til then. To see the neighbor kids runnin' around, nothin' but skin and bone, their eyes sunk in, their bellies big with hunger, made us thankful we only had ourselves."

Hank picked up a carrot and started peeling again. "Then came the dust," he went on. "The soil got so dry it turned into powder, and the wind blew hot and angry, day after day. Got so dark we had to light lamps in the middle of the day, and we forgot there used to be stars at night. Dust was everywhere. We soaked towels to try and keep it from creepin' under the doors and windowsills, but it got in anyway. We ate it, we breathed it, we wore it, day and night."

Hank peeled faster. "The fields all disappeared. Weren't nothin' left but acres and acres of black, shiftin' sand, drifts deep enough to bury a cow or a child that got caught out unawares.

"Before long Lisbeth's cough started. Lots of folks have it back home. They cough up dust and then more dust, thick and black, and then they start coughin' up blood. Ain't no money for doctorin', so it just gets worse and worse.

"Last October the bank came and took our farm away. We watched them auction it off, Lisbeth and I, and then Lisbeth sank down in the dust and coughed herself to death."

Hank stopped and stood silent, his face like stone, the glimmer of a tear in the corner of his eye. I turned away, swallowing down the lump in my throat, forcing back the tears that threatened to spill from my eyes, too.

"Welp," said Hank, clearing his throat and busying himself with the vegetables again. "Not doin' much of a job at cheerin' folks up, am I?"

I looked at him and we both gave a half-hearted laugh.

"That's better," he said.

We finished cooking and brought Mama out to the kitchen. Then, after we'd eaten and tucked Maureen in, Hank and Ma started swapping tales, Okie and Irish. Hank got Mama laughing so hard that her eyes shone and pink came back to her cheeks. Sitting around the table like that, laughing and talking, I forgot for a moment that Pa wasn't there and that we weren't a whole family anymore.

Then, when I remembered again, I got so mad at myself that I snapped at Mama. "I hate to spoil your fun," I told her. "But it's almost nine o'clock. Don't you think *he* oughta go?"

The laughter drained from Mama's eyes and she blushed a deep pink. "Daniel," she said, "that's very rude. Please apologize to Mr. Powers."

"No, ma'am," said Hank. "The boy's right. It's time I was goin'."

He said goodnight and went out the kitchen door. Hank never goes through the bedrooms. We heard the front door open and close, then Mama turned to me.

"That wasn't very nice, Daniel," she said. "What's got into you?"

"What's got into *you?*" I said. "Actin' so lousy all the time, never laughing, never singing anymore? The only time you seem happy is when *he's* around. And how come you don't write to Pa anymore?"

Ma's eyes filled with sorrow. She put her head down in her hands and sighed. Suddenly I felt like such a dumbbell. I'd asked Hank over to cheer her up, and now I'd gone and made her sad again. What was wrong with me anyway?

"I'm sorry," I said. "It was my idea for Hank to come. I don't know why I got mad like that."

Mama looked up. "I know what you're feelin', Danny," she said quietly. "I'm feeling it, too. But there's no sin in enjoying Hank's company. We're all just lonely souls, giving each other a bit of comfort."

I nodded. "I know, Ma," I said. "Come on. I'll help you to bed."

I slid my arm under her shoulders and helped her to her feet. She leaned against me, then looked up and smiled.

"My, yer gettin' big and strong," she said. "Wasn't it just last fall I could kiss the top of yer head?"

I smiled and nodded. It's true. I don't know how many inches I've grown over the winter, but I am taller than Mama now.

"Won't Pa be surprised when he gets home?" I said.

Mama looked at me. It seemed for a moment that

she was about to say something, but then she looked away.

"Aye," she said softly.

I helped her into bed and tucked the covers around her the way she'd done for me so many times. Her stomach is so big and round, and the rest of her so pale and thin, that it seems like the baby is some kind of little monster, eating her up from the inside. I wish it would hurry up and get born. I don't care if it lives or dies. I guess that's a sin, but I don't care. I just want it to leave Mama alone.

FORTY-ONE

~~~~~~~~~

Friday, April 28, 1933

I finally managed to pry Mickey away from Kitty long enough to get a stickball game together after school. It was cold and damp out, but it still felt great to be with the guys again, just like old times.

Mama was propped up in her rocker when I got home. She seemed to be having a hard time breathing.

"You all right, Ma?" I asked her.

"Aye," she said, "just tired. Do me a favor and take Maureen out for a breath of air before supper. Poor child has forgotten there's a world beyond that door."

I did as Mama said and took Maureen down to the park for a while. It was growing colder as the evening came on. It's been a raw April, more like March. I keep hoping the warm weather will come, both for Pa's sake, wherever he is, and to help cheer

Mama up. Folks are saying, though, that we'll likely go straight from winter to summer with no spring at all this year.

I pushed Maureen on the swing for a time. Then I put her down and she chased pigeons and I chased her until we were both chilled through and exhausted.

Mama was in bed when we got back, her face gray, her breath coming heavy.

"Mama? What's wrong?"

She bit her lip and looked at me with frightened eyes. "Oh, Daniel," she said. "I fear it's begun."

My heart banged against my chest.

"What's begun?" I asked hoarsely.

"The baby. The baby is coming and it's too soon, near a month too soon." She closed her eyes and tears squeezed out from under her lashes.

I took a deep breath and willed my heart to stop pounding.

"It'll be all right, Mama," I told her. "I'll get the doctor. It'll be all right."

I yelled for Hank, but he wasn't home yet, so I ran over and got Mrs. Riley and the girls. Then I took off after Doc. He wasn't in, but his wife said she expected him any minute and would I care to wait? I felt like saying I wouldn't care to wait at all, but I guessed that wouldn't help matters much. I sat down and flipped through the pages of some magazine, even though I was too nervous to see what I was looking at.

The room was cluttered with books and doilies,

and it smelled of furniture polish. There was a big brown clock on the wall that ticked real loud. I watched the hands move. With every minute that passed it seemed I could feel the blood racing faster through my veins. Five minutes, ten, fifteen. My head felt like it was going to burst. I got up and started pacing. Five more minutes passed. I started to sweat. Where on earth could he be? At least Mrs. Davis walked back into the room.

"Hasn't he come back yet?" she asked.

"No," I shouted. "Look, I gotta find him. Where did he go?"

"Well, he had a number of calls to make. Is this an emergency, young man?"

"Yes, it's an emergency. My ma's having a baby!"

"Oh well, then, if that's all—"

"What do you mean, if that's all!"

Mrs. Davis smiled and shook her head. "You men get so worked up over these things. It's the most natural thing in the world. Why I remember when Mrs. Flaherty—"

"Mrs. Davis, please . . . you don't understand. I've got to find Doc *now!*"

"All right, all right. I'll tell you where he went. But I'll let you in on a little secret. Your mama will probably go right ahead and have her baby just fine, with or without Doc."

She was writing as she spoke, and when she finished she handed me a list of addresses. I grabbed it from her hand and tore out of the room without even bothering to say thanks. Down on the street I checked the list. Chances are she copied it right out of the appointment book in order, I figured, so if I started with the last one first, that's probably where he'd be.

It turned out that Mrs. Davis had more brains than I'd given her credit for and had already reversed the list. That still didn't help, though, because Doc apparently followed his own route which had nothing to do with order whatsoever. I ended up going to all four addresses only to find that Doc had been and gone and apparently was on his way back home again.

Nearly frantic and sweating like crazy, I stood once again banging furiously on Doc's door. It had been over an hour now since I'd left Ma. Anything could have happened. At last the door swung open.

"All right, all right," said Mrs. Davis. "Oh, it's you again. Doc just left. Didn't you pass him in the hall?"

"Left! Left where?"

"Why to see your mother, of course. Why didn't you tell me it was an emergency?"

I stared at her, so frustrated I didn't know whether to cry or scream. I just shook my head and bolted after Doc. I caught up with him on the next block. Boy, was he hopping mad!

"Why didn't you call me sooner?" he shouted.

"Sooner! Where do you think I've been? Chasing you all over the dad-blamed city, that's where!"

"Did you call the hospital?"

"What hospital?"

"The Fifth Avenue, of course!"

"No, I didn't call the hospital. You didn't say anything about any hospital. You said to call *you*."

"Well, can't you use your brain, boy? Your mother's a sick woman."

"Don't you think I know that?"

Doc didn't answer. We had reached our building and he was taking the steps two at a time. When he reached the door he burst right through and stalked into Mama's room without a word to anyone.

Mrs. Riley stood leaning against the sink, a cup of tea in her hand. "And a good day to you, too, Doctor," she called after him. She turned and gave me a wink. "You've got a little brother," she said, just as calm as if she was saying *the mail came* or *there's beans for supper.* "And," she added, "your Mama is fine."

My knees suddenly started trembling and I knew that if I didn't sit down I was gonna fall down. Mrs. Riley knew it, too, I guess, because she suddenly rushed over and slid a chair under me.

"There, there," she said. "You've had quite a scare, haven't you, poor thing?"

"Mama's all right?" I whispered.

"Just fine."

"A brother?"

"A lovely little brother—a bit scrawny, but he'll fill out."

"And it's all over, just like that?"

"Just like that."

Doc Davis came out into the kitchen a few minutes later, looking like he'd just been robbed.

FORTY-TWO

"She's still going to the hospital," Doc insisted, shaking his finger at Mrs. Riley.

"I am *not!*" came Mama's voice from the bedroom.

Mrs. Riley smiled. "Go on," she said, pushing me toward the bedroom door. "Go meet your brother. I'll talk to the good doctor."

Mama was propped up on a couple of pillows. She looked tired, but happy. She smiled at me and reached out her arms. I hugged her tight.

"I love you, Danny," she whispered.

"I love you, too, Mama. Are you sure you're okay?"

"Just fine. You've got a brother." She pointed to the Rileys' old cradle on the other side of the bed. I went around and peeked in.

"He's little," I said.

"Aye. So were you once."

"That little?"

"Well, not quite. He's a bit early, but Doc says he'll catch up. You can pick him up. He won't break."

I bent down and picked the little fella up. He was as floppy as a rag doll.

"His head. Watch his head," Mama warned.

"I know," I told her, sliding my elbow under his head. "It wasn't so long ago Maureen was new."

Mama smiled. "I guess I'm forgettin' how grown-up you are."

I looked down at the baby. He was all puffy and pink, with a mass of curly black hair that clung in damp ringlets around his face. He was warm in my arms, and I felt sorry for the things I'd thought about him the past few weeks. I was glad he was okay. He held his hands clenched in two tight fists, like a tiny prizefighter ready to take on the world. I poked at one of the fists and five tiny fingers fanned out, then closed again over mine.

"Got a good grip," I said.

At the sound of my voice, he opened his eyes and stared up into my face.

"He's lookin' at me," I said.

"Sure he is," said Mama. "And I'm bettin' he can see you, too, no matter what the old wives say."

"Sure he can. See the way he's wrinkling up his nose? He's thinking, 'Gee, I hope I'm not related to this funny-looking guy.' "

Mama laughed. "He's not thinkin' any such thing, now."

I looked at the little face again, and suddenly felt a twinge of jealousy. "He's the image of Pa," I said. "It's him should be Daniel junior, not me."

Mama's eyes filled with tears and she looked away.

"Mama, I'm sorry. I didn't mean to make you sad."

"No, it's all right." Mama brushed her tears away. "Come on over here, the both of ya."

I carried the baby around and sat down on the side of the bed. Mama reached up and grabbed my chin.

"Now, you listen," she said sternly. "I don't ever want to hear you talkin' like that again. You are yer daddy's firstborn son. He gave you his name, and it belongs to you. You remind me more of him every day."

I made a face, thinking she was just giving me a line, but Mama shook her head and went on.

"I'm not speakin' of yer features or the color of yer hair. I'm speakin' of yer heart, Danny, and yer courage. The way you're growin' to be a man. You are yer daddy's son, all right, and you've done nothing but proud by his name."

I smiled, warmed by her words.

"Besides," she went on, "this little bairn's got a name of 'is own—Padraic."

"Padraic?"

"Aye." Mama beamed. "It was *my* father's name."

"I know that, Mama . . . but—"

"But what?"

"Well, don't you think it sounds sort of . . . Irish?"

Mama's eyes flew open wide.

"And what were you expectin' then? Jewish? Or Spanish, maybe?"

"No, Mama, American."

"American?"

"Yes, Ma. We *are* American."

"Aye, that we are, but . . ." Mama's eyes grew troubled. "Are ya wantin' so soon to forget yer Irish roots?"

"No, Ma, of course not. I'm proud to be Irish. It's just that the kids'll give him an awful hard time with a name like Padraic."

Mama stared at me a moment longer, then brushed the baby's cheek with her finger and smiled.

"So," she said, "yer big brother is lookin' out for ya already. What do ya think of that?"

The baby yawned and closed his eyes.

"Aye," said Mama, "sleep well. You're in good hands."

She looked up at me.

"American it is then," she said. "*Patrick*. Patrick Seamus Garvey."

"Seamus?"

"Something wrong with Seamus, too?"

"Nope, nope. Seamus is fine."

"Don't worry," I whispered as I tucked Patrick back into his cradle. "Nobody ever uses their middle name anyway."

FORTY-THREE

When Doc left, the score stood tied, Doc–one, Ma–one. Doc had agreed not to make Ma go to the hospital as long as Ma agreed not to try to nurse Patrick.

"You're too weak," he told her, "and the baby will thrive just as well on cows' milk."

"Aye," grumbled Mama, "and pigs can fly." But she gave in.

It was late by the time we got everyone settled, and I fell into bed, exhausted. Tired as I was, though, I jumped up again in the middle of the night as soon as Patrick started to cry. We had moved Maureen's crib into my room, but still, I was afraid Patrick might wake her. Besides, I figured I could give Patrick his bottle and let Mama rest. I guessed she was exhausted, too, 'cause she never moved a muscle when I went in to pick up the baby. I whisked him out to the kitchen and popped the little sugar teat Maggie had made for him into his mouth to keep him quiet while I heated his milk.

A soft knock came on the door, and I opened it to find Hank standing there.

"Heard the little feller hollerin'," he said. "Figured you might need a hand."

"Can you change a diaper?" I asked.

"Reckon I can. I was second oldest of fourteen kids."

"Whew! And I thought Rileys were a crowd."

Hank laid Patrick on the table and started undoing his pins.

"He sure is a puny one, ain't he? How's your ma?"

"Okay, I guess. She's still sleeping."

Hank looked at me and raised an eyebrow. "Sleepin'?"

"Yeah."

"You mean she didn't wake up with this little feller hollerin'?"

"No," I said, my stomach starting to squeeze into a knot. "I . . . guess she's real tired."

Hank pushed his hair back and scratched his head. He looked troubled. "Never heard of a mother so tired she didn't hear her newborned baby cry," he said. "I better just check in on her."

"No, no, I'll check," I said, trying to keep my voice steady. "I'm sure she's fine."

I tiptoed back into Mama's room and over to the bed. Her face looked small and pale, lost in the tangle of red hair that spread out over her pillow. One leg hung down over the side of the bed, as if she had thought to get up, then changed her mind. The blanket covered her chest and I stood stone still, staring at it, waiting to see it rise and fall. A second went by, two, ten, an eternity, and still the blanket did not rise. Trembling, I placed my hand in front of her open mouth. I held my own breath, waiting. It seemed forever. Then, at last, there was a rush of warm air.

I breathed again myself—deeply, with relief—then moved my hand up and rested it on her forehead. It was damp and cold.

"Mama?" I whispered.

There was no response.

"Mama? Are you sleeping?"

Still no response. I stepped forward and leaned in closer. My leg bumped into Mama's, and I felt something wet and sticky beneath my toes. I looked down. There was a small, dark puddle on the floor. My heart thudded against my chest at the sight of it. My hand shook as I reached out to pull the blanket back.

"Oh God," I breathed. "Oh, *God!* Hank! Come quick!"

FORTY-FOUR

Saturday, April 29, 1933

Doc stormed out of the operating room in a blind
rage.

"I told her!" he shouted. "I told her. What a waste.
What a damned waste!"

"Doctor!" One of the nurses gave Doc a sharp,
silencing look, then nodded toward the bench where
Hank and I sat waiting. Doc shook his head in dis-
gust and walked over to us. He looked at Hank,
looked at me, then motioned Hank to one side.

"No." I stood up. "She's *my* mother. Tell me."

Doc studied my face again, then nodded.

"Your mother's lost a lot of blood," he said, "and
she was very weak to begin with. She's in a coma.
Do you know what a coma is?"

I shook my head.

"It means her brain was deprived of oxygen for

some time and is now functioning only on a rudimentary level."

"What does that mean?" I asked.

"It means she can breathe, and that's about it."

Doc's harsh words and manner were hard to take, but I had to know more.

"Will she get better?" I asked.

"Better. Or worse," said Doc.

I stared at him. If I asked the next question I had to be ready for the answer, and I wasn't sure I was ready yet. If only Pa were here. Where on earth was Pa?

Hank put a hand on my shoulder..

"You okay, son?" he asked.

I jerked away from his touch. "Of course I'm okay, and I'm not your son." I glared at Doc. "So what are you saying?" I asked. "Is she gonna die?"

"I don't know."

"What do you mean you don't know? What kind of answer is that? You're the doctor."

"That's right. I'm the doctor. Not God. I've done all I can. If you're a believer, you can pray. If not, all you can do is wait."

"How long?"

Doc shrugged. "Days, weeks, months maybe, though I doubt she could hang on that long. There's just no telling."

"What . . . What will she be like if she lives?"

"No tellin' that, either," said Doc. "Don't know how serious the oxygen deprivation was. She could be normal. She could be . . . not much better than she is right now."

It was all too much. I slumped back down on the bench.

"You might as well go on home now," Doc said.

I looked up at him. "Home? You mean, just leave her here? What if something happens? What if she needs me?"

"If there's any change, we'll call you."

"But . . . I *can't* go home."

"Look, son," said Doc. "I'll tell you once more. This can go on for weeks or even months. You *can't* stay here."

"Can I just see her, then?"

"Not today, maybe tomorrow." Doc started walking away.

"Please?" I called after him.

"Tomorrow!" he shouted over his shoulder.

Hank patted me on the back.

"Come on, boy," he said gently. "We'd better go."

We rode down the elevator in silence, walked through the dark, cool corridors, and stepped out into bright, blinding sunshine. I realized, bitterly, that spring had come at last. It was the kind of morning on which Mama would rush through the house, throwing the windows open and singing, "When Irish eyes are smiling, sure it's like a morn in spring. . . ."

Would Mama ever sing again?

"Go home," Doc had said. Where was home? The apartment? The apartment was just four walls and a floor. An empty box. It needed Pa's laughter to make it home. It needed Ma's singing to make it home. Who could I turn to now?

"Do you believe in God, Hank?"

"Yep."

"Why?"

"Insurance."

"Insurance?"

"Yep."

"What's that supposed to mean?"

Hank pushed back his hair.

"Welp," he said, "the way I figure it, you can either believe in God or not. If you believe in God and it turns out there is a God, you're all set. And if you believe in God, and it turns out there's not a God, you haven't lost much. *But,* if you don't believe in God, and it turns out there *is* a God, welp, I wouldn't wanna be in your shoes, buddy." He looked at me and grinned.

I frowned in return. "I'm not kidding around, Hank."

Hank's smile disappeared and he ran his hand through his hair again. "Yeah," he said. "I know. It's just that it ain't easy for a guy like me to explain. But there's more to folks than bone and blood, I know that much. And there's more to this world than meets the eye."

"*How* do you know, Hank? Don't you ever have doubts?"

"Oh shore. Shore I do." His face grew grave. "Times like these I have plenty of doubts. Wouldn't be human if I didn't. But I always come back to

259

believin'. Somebody out there cares about homely old Hank. I just feel it, in here." Hank put his big, callused hand over his heart.

"I wish I could feel it," I told him.

"You will, son. You will." Hank slid his arm around my shoulders. This time I let it stay.

FORTY-FIVE

I lay awake far into the night. I guess I was afraid to go to sleep. It seemed like by staying awake and keeping Ma in my mind I could keep her alive somehow. If I fell asleep she might slip away.

I turned Doc's words over and over. "Days, weeks, months . . ." I've been waiting so long for Pa, every minute thinking maybe today, maybe tomorrow; sitting on the front stoop staring at the corner, thinking, maybe the next man, maybe the next. . . . How can I wait for Ma now, too?

Suddenly I couldn't. I couldn't lie there and wait one more minute. Every muscle, every nerve in my body screamed, "Do something!" But what? What could I do?

Then I knew. I would go find Pa. Now. Tonight. I would bring him back, and he would make Ma live. I knew he would.

I got up and dressed silently, fighting back waves of fear. What if Ma needed me while I was gone? What if—I couldn't let myself think about that. I had to go. I had to find Pa. I got out the things I'd hidden to take along when I went: Pa's watch and some old photographs. I wrapped them in a bundle with some extra clothes.

I bent over Maureen's crib, touched my fingers to my lips, then brushed her cheek. "You'll be okay," I whispered. "Hank will take good care of you 'til I get back. I'm going to find Pa."

She stirred softly and I tucked her blanket close around her. I looked toward Mama's room. I would have liked to kiss Patrick good-bye, too, but Hank was sleeping in there to keep an eye on him, and I couldn't take the chance. I blew a kiss toward the door instead, then tiptoed through the front room and silently let myself out. I stood there a moment in the semidarkness of the hall, staring up at the cold, white moon outside the window. I looked back at the door. How could I leave them all — Ma, Maureen, Patrick — one more helpless than the other?

Then I thought of Maggie. Strong, capable Maggie. Maggie wouldn't let anything go wrong while I was away. I tiptoed over and knocked lightly on her door. There was no answer. I knocked again, and this time I heard a soft scuffling.

"Who is it?" came a sleepy voice.

"Shush," I whispered, "it's Danny. Open up."

The latch slid over and the knob turned, then Maggie stepped out into the hall in her nightgown.

262

"What is it?" she asked, her eyes scrunched up in concern. "Is it your ma?"

I shook my head quickly and motioned her farther out into the hall. She pulled the door silently shut behind her and walked with me over to the window. She glanced down at the sack in my hand and her expression hardened.

"You're running away?" she said.

"I'm not running away," I whispered. "I'm going to find Pa."

Maggie stared at me for a long moment, then slowly shook her head. "You're running away," she repeated, "just like my pa, just like yours."

"My pa didn't run away," I told her angrily. "And neither did yours. Your ma threw him out. I saw her."

Maggie turned and stared out the window. "My pa ran away years ago," she said. "He ran away into a whiskey bottle."

I stood there a moment, collecting my thoughts.

"Maybe so," I said, "but *my* pa didn't run away."

Maggie looked at me again. "Maybe not," she said. "Maybe he left for a reason, but you've got no reason. Why are you going?"

"I've got to find him."

"You'll never find him. He could be anywhere."

"I don't care. I've got to try."

"Why?"

"Because."

"Because why?"

I turned away and stared out the window at the

263

train tracks across the street. I felt confused and angry. Why did Maggie have to mix me up this way? I wished I were out there in the night, and I wished the train would come along and take me away—away from Maggie's questions, away from Mama's hospital bed, away from Patrick's helplessness, away from Maureen's cries of "Mama." I felt suddenly weak, and I leaned forward until my face pressed against the cool glass. I closed my eyes and listened in my head to the rhythm of the train wheels I'd heard all my life. *Away,* they said, *away, away, away, away.* . . .

There was a soft touch on my arm.

"It's not out there," Maggie whispered.

"What?"

"What you're looking for."

"I told you I'm looking for Pa."

"Are you?"

"Yes! Will you leave me alone?" I closed my eyes and angry tears squeezed out beneath my lids. *No,* said a voice inside me, a quiet voice, growing louder. *No, you're not looking for Pa. Not anymore. Maggie's right. That's just an excuse. You* are *running away.*

The anger melted into sorrow and I put my bundle down on the windowsill and stared up at the ceiling.

"So what am I looking for?" I asked.

"The strength," said Maggie, "to face tomorrow."

The truth of her words brought fresh tears to my eyes.

"And where do I find it?"

"Right here," said Maggie, "at home."

"What home?"

"This home." Maggie reached out and pulled me into the warm circle of her arms. "Our home."

FORTY-SIX

Sunday, April 30, 1933

I awoke with a start, angry at myself for having fallen asleep after all, and praying that Ma was okay. It was so early that the babies were still sleeping, but the sound of pots and pans rattling in the kitchen told me that Hank was up. My bundle still sat at the foot of the bed. I unpacked it quickly so Hank wouldn't see. I carried the watch and pictures back to Mama's room. I wouldn't be needing them anymore.

When I went to put Pa's watch back in Ma's dresser, Ma's bundle of unsent letters slid sideways and I saw something familiar behind them. Pa's wallet. *Pa's wallet!* What was that doing here? Surely he must have taken it with him. I lifted it out and opened it. An oversized envelope was folded up and sandwiched inside. It was smudged, like it had been rained on, but I could still read it. It was addressed to Ma, and there was a letter inside.

A strange sense of dread came over me as I held it in my hand, and I trembled at the thought of reading it. Maybe I shouldn't, I told myself. It was, after all, addressed to Ma. But I was only stalling. Having found it, I could do nothing else but read it. At last I found the courage to slide it from its envelope and unfold it.

Dear Mrs. Garvey,

It pains me greatly to have to write this letter, but I'm afraid there is no help for it. I have grievous news.

Our husbands, it seems, was riding a freight together back in December. They was coming into a station and had to jump train so the railroad bulls wouldn't catch them. Your husband slipped. He was killed instantly. I'm sorry. Harold, my husband, says he didn't suffer if that's any comfort.

What happened next I can hardly bring myself to write. Harold stole your husband's wallet. Please don't hate him Mrs. Garvey. Harold is a good, Christian man. It was hunger and desperation that drove him to it. He's been carrying the wallet ever since, sick at heart over what he done. When he got home yesterday he asked me to send it to you right away and beg your forgiveness. He would have wrote you hisself, but he don't know how.

Howard says your husband was a fine man
and loved his family powerful. He was on his
way home for Christmas when it happened.
God bless you.

Sincerely,
Hannah Bartlett

PS: The wallet was empty.

I read back over the one line that meant so much. "He was on his way home for Christmas when it happened." *He was on his way home.*

I closed my eyes and let the tears fall. It hurt, but not as bad as I'd expected. Maybe I was just numb, or maybe I had already done my grieving a thousand times—every time a knock on the door had turned out to be someone else, every time the footsteps in the hall had gone on by, every time I'd run up behind a big, dark-haired man on the street only to find a stranger's face looking back. Maybe you can only lose someone so many times.

I turned the envelope over and looked at the post date, April second. Mama had known, then, for two or three weeks. No wonder she'd been acting so strange. If only she'd told me. I could've helped her. I could've shared the burden.

I walked out into the kitchen and put the wallet down on the table. Hank was bent over the stove.

"My pa is dead," I said.

Hank froze in the middle of pouring milk into Patrick's bottle. He lowered the pan and looked at me. His eyes were filled with sorrow.

"I know," he said gently.

It took a moment for the full meaning of his words to sink in. Then, when it did, a surge of white-hot anger rushed through my veins.

"You knew? What do you mean you *knew?* She told *you,* and she didn't tell *me!*"

Hank still held Patrick's bottle in his hand. I ran over and grabbed it away.

"What's going on here?" I shouted. "What was happening between you two? You're probably *glad* Pa's dead."

Hank grabbed my shoulders.

"Now, you listen here," he told me. "It weren't nothin' like that and you know it. I was just here the day the letter came is all. Your ma asked me to look into the insurance. She was gonna tell you. She just wanted to wait 'til after the baby came. She said you had enough on your mind."

I pulled away from him.

"I don't believe you," I shouted. It felt good to have someone to scream at. "You're lying! I've heard what the neighbors are saying. I've been a fool not to know you and Ma were carrying on. I *hate* you, Hank Powers. You're nothin' but a . . . a gigolo!"

Hank stared at me, his eyes narrowed, his breath coming fast and angry. Gradually his chest stopped heaving and he shook his head.

"If you weren't hurtin' so bad," he said, "I'd whoop you good for what you just said about your ma. Now if you'll just calm down and get your head on straight, you'll recognize that your ma ain't been in a condition to 'carry on' with anybody of late. And as for me being a gigolo. Welp . . ." He started to smile. "It'd be nice work if I could get it, but I ask you honestly now, is this the face of a gigolo?"

I looked into his big, homely face, and all the anger drained out of me. I smiled in spite of myself.

"I'm sorry, Hank," I said, the tears starting in again. "It's just that . . ."

"I know what it is, son. I know what it is."

FORTY-SEVEN

~~~~~~~

Saturday, June 10, 1933

In the beginning I had plenty of company at the hospital. Maggie came, and Mickey, Mrs. Riley, Mrs. Mahoney, and lots of the neighbors. Even old Mr. Weissman came a few times. As the weeks went by, though, people got busy with their lives again. Now it's just me, and occasionally Hank or Maggie, but mostly just me.

Hank has mentioned a couple of times that we should have a funeral Mass for Pa. But I can't. Not yet. Not without Ma.

I sit with her every day after school and hold her hand. I tell her stories and jokes. I read her favorite books out loud and sing her favorite songs. I tell her all about Maureen and Patrick. And she lies there, never moving, never smiling, never opening her eyes. She's gotten thinner and paler. Her mouth is just a narrow blue line and her eyes are sunken gray hollows above her cheeks.

Doc Davis came in and found me with her this afternoon. I was reading from *Black Beauty*. He smiled when he saw me. I don't think I've ever seen him smile before. He pulled up Mama's eyelids and looked into her eyes with a little light. Then he felt her pulse and listened to her heart.

"How is she, Doc?" I asked.

"Weaker."

"How much longer can she go on?"

Doc sighed and spoke to me more gently than I've ever heard him speak.

"Son," he said, "I don't know what's kept her alive this long."

I looked down at my book. Doc came over and put a hand on my shoulder.

"Why don't you go out and get some fresh air," he said. "A boy your age should be playing stickball on a nice day like this."

"That's okay," I said. "I'd rather be here."

"She doesn't even know you're here."

"I know."

Doc shook his head and went out. A short time later a nurse came in.

"Visiting hours are over for the afternoon, Master Garvey," she said. "You'll have to leave now."

"I'll be right out," I told her.

She went out and left me alone again.

I got up and kissed Mama's cheek, then I leaned in close to her ear.

"Mama," I whispered, "it's me, Danny. I'm here. Please know that I'm here. I'm waiting for you—me and Maureen and Patrick. We love you, Mama. We need you. Please let us be enough."

She just lay there, still as death.

Hank had dinner waiting when I got home. Beans and franks. I no sooner sat down than a knock came on the door. It was Angela, Mrs. DeLuca's little daughter from down at the candy store. She stared up at me timidly with her huge, brown eyes, and I had the feeling that if I'd said, "Boo," she would have turned and fled.

"Yes, Angela?" I asked gently.

She held up her hand and counted her message off on her fingers as she spoke.

"Mama says the hospital called." One finger down. "She says there's been a change." Second finger down. "And you better come quick." Third finger down. A fourth finger was still sticking up.

"Anything else?" I asked.

She stuck the last finger into her mouth and thought for a moment, then shook her head. My heart sank.

"Thank you," I said, the words coming out like a croak. The message was painfully clear. If it had been good news the caller would have said so. Nobody likes to give bad news over the phone. For a moment steel jaws seemed to close over my heart 'til I thought I would crumble with the pain. Then, mercifully, a numbing fog descended, and I felt nothing at all.

I turned to look at Hank. He seemed far away, like I was seeing him through the wrong end of a telescope. His face was twisted in sorrow.

"Well," I said tiredly, "at least the waiting is over."

"I'll come with you," said Hank's faraway voice.

"No. I want to go alone."

"All right," said Hank. A tear slid down his cheek. "But remember, I'm here for you, boy. You call if you need me."

I walked the two blocks to the hospital with the thick fog swirling around me. I saw nothing but Mama's face. My body must have stopped at the stoplights, crossed the streets, opened the doors, and spoken to the elevator operator, but it did all those things without any direction from me.

The nurse at the nursing station said something as I went by, but her words did not penetrate the fog. I pushed open the door to Mama's room and stood there, trying to focus. Mama's shrunken body lay facedown on the bed, naked to the waist, covered by a sheet below. Two nurses bent over her, lifting the limp arms and gently washing. They looked up sharply when I came in.

"Master Garvey!" said one. "Please wait in the hall. You've *no right* to be in here just now."

Suddenly there was a quiver, a flicker of movement from the bed. My heart stood still, and I watched in fear and wonder as the withered arms jerked and drew in against the still body. Then slowly, miraculously, like the sun rising up out of the darkness, Mama's head lifted from the pillow. She turned and looked directly at me, her eyes open and shining, a trembling smile on her lips.

"Aye, he does," she whispered. "Aye. He does."

"Mama!"

FORTY-EIGHT

June—1934

As soon as Ma was well enough, the neighbors all pitched in and we gave Pa the grandest funeral ever. It did our hearts good to see how many people came. I'm sure Pa could feel the love, all the way up to heaven.

It's funny to think that, in a way, Pa ended up providing for us after all. That insurance policy that I've cursed so many times has been enough to see us through. We're not rich, but between the insurance, my shoeshine business, and Hank, we're doing okay. Mr. Roosevelt's New Deal is working, and the depression is slowly getting better, but I know now that it's going to take a long time. Longer than I ever dreamed.

More than a year has passed since the winter of 1933, but I'll never forget it. If I grow up to be the richest man in the world, I will still remember how it feels to be hungry, to have to beg, and I'll never look down on anyone who's fallen on hard times.

Which reminds me, I ran into Sadie the other day. She said her bank did open up again and she got all her money back.

"Did you take it out and put it under your mattress?" I asked her.

"No." She laughed her wonderful warm laugh. "I was tempted to, honey. I admit that. But I figure we got to start somewhere to trust again."

I guess if a depression had heroes, the way wars do, Sadie would be one. And so would Ma and Hank and Mrs. Riley and all the other ordinary people who keep on trying and keep on trusting.

Ma and Hank got married this morning, which made it a real red-letter day for the neighborhood busybodies. There hasn't been as much winking and nodding and saying "I told you so," since the day that one of the two old bachelors on the first floor locked the other one out in the hall in a lady's nightgown.

When Ma and Hank first told me they were getting married, I was pretty sore. But I couldn't stay mad. I've seen the way Hank has stood by Mama this whole year, caring for her and supporting her. I guess it's no surprise that their friendship has grown into love. Besides, Mama says her love for Hank won't ever take the place of her love for Pa. She says she will always love Pa, just the way Hank will always love Elizabeth, but that they still have love enough left over for each other. Mama says that's the wonder of love. You never run out of it. I know what she's telling me is true, too, because I kind of feel the same way about Pa and Hank myself.

It's a funny thing about Hank. The longer you know him, the better-looking he seems to get. Mama says it's the beauty inside him shining through, and I guess maybe there's got to be some truth in that.

The wedding was small. Just us and the Rileys, Mrs. Mahoney, and, of course, Mickey. Ma and Hank asked Maggie and me to stand up for them. Maggie looked beautiful. She had on a new pink dress and a wreath of little white flowers in her hair. I snuck a peek at her just as Ma and Hank were saying "I do," and I caught her sneaking a peak at me, too. It was like Mickey says, *copacetic*.

Hank is going to adopt Maureen and Patrick. I wasn't too crazy about that idea at first, but I'm getting used to it. Nobody could ever love them any more than Hank does, that's for sure. And I guess it'll be less confusing for them growing up if they have the same name as Ma and Hank. Ma and I tell them stories about Pa all the time so they'll never forget who he was, and about Ireland so they'll never forget who they are. Mama says I'm getting to be a bit of a *seanachie* myself.

Hank wanted to adopt me, too, but I said no. After all, I'm fifteen now, near a grown man myself. I'm just as big as Pa was and almost as strong. I even have to shave. Besides, my name is Daniel Tomas Garvey. It was my Daddy's name, and his Daddy's name before him. It's a good name, and that's the one thing no one can ever take away from me.

GREAT
EPISODES

Other titles now available:

TIMMY O'DOWD AND THE BIG DITCH
by Len Hilts
•
JENNY OF THE TETONS
by Kristiana Gregory
•
THE RIDDLE OF PENNCROFT FARM
by Dorothea Jensen
•
THE LEGEND OF JIMMY SPOON
by Kristiana Gregory
•
GUNS FOR GENERAL WASHINGTON
by Seymour Reit
•
UNDERGROUND MAN
by Milton Meltzer
•
A RIDE INTO MORNING:
THE STORY OF TEMPE WICK
by Ann Rinaldi

Look for exciting new titles to come in the Great
Episodes series of historical fiction.